BUCK COWBOYS

BUCK COWBOYS #1

ELLE THORPE

WWW.ELLETHORPE.COM

#1

For my mum.

You're the strongest woman I know, and I'm so proud to be your daughter.

So many of my female characters are inspired by you, qualities you possess, or things you've taught me.

Thank you for always having my back, even if you still can't bring yourself to read my books. I swear, the sex scenes aren't that bad! (Okay, they are.) Hahaha.

I love you.

Elle x

1

HALLIE

"Oh, hell no. Not today, Satan." Digging the heels of my boots into the scuffed hardwood floor, I hauled ass to the doorway I'd just walked through. It didn't matter that the band was playing my song and I was itching to shake off the dust on the dance floor. It didn't matter that after working at the ranch all week, my throat was parched and craving an ice-cold beer.

All that mattered was bright blue eyes I'd recognize anywhere, even through the dimly lit crowd having Friday night drinks at the Black Bull Bar.

Summer caught me by the shoulders, halting my escape. "Whoa." She pointed at her chest. "It's Summer, not Satan. Though you've called me worse, I suppose."

I none-too-softly jabbed an elbow into her midsection. "Not you, dope. Him. It. Gah. Just no." I swiveled for the door again, but I was cut off by the group of cowboys Summer and her dad were training, so I had no choice but to get swept along in the mass of large male bodies.

Normally, I wouldn't have minded. It wasn't much of a hardship, being pressed between fit young guys, who had the rhythm and coordination, not to mention the balls to get on the back of a bull and try to ride him for eight seconds. No, normally, I'd be laughing and chatting up a storm. That was who I was. Hallie Ryan. Life of the party. One of the guys. Always up for a joke and a good time.

But that was before I'd seen Nathaniel Mathews' baby blues from beneath a battered baseball cap.

And he'd noticed me, too.

Summer squinted into the smoky bar, and I knew the moment she realized who I was talking about. Her fingers pressed into the skin of my arm, and she dragged me to a table in the corner of the room.

It wasn't far enough away.

I could still see him, even though I tried my best not to look in his direction. His gaze still burned across my skin, following my every move. I sank down into the wooden chair, catching my balance as it wobbled on uneven legs.

Summer peered at me, her big brown eyes filled with sympathy. "You didn't know he was back in town?"

That got my attention. "You did?"

Summer shrugged. "Dad said he was visiting his sister before the next leg of his tour. Supposed to only be a few days. Was kind of hoping you wouldn't hear about it."

I glared at her. "You're fired as my best friend. I was not emotionally or mentally prepared for this. Like, fuck. He never comes home. Why now?"

She lifted one shoulder, but then Austin pulled up the seat beside her, and she was too busy kissing her boyfriend hello to pay attention my woes. They launched into a discussion about their days, but unfortunately, listening to the drone of their 'been together too long' conversation was not at all a diversion from the man across the bar. I couldn't help but sneak another glance at him.

Aaaaand he was still staring at me. Shit. I was completely busted. Our gazes clashed, and that longtime spark I'd fought so hard to bury lit right the fuck up, just like it had four years ago.

Nope. No way. Not doing that again.

I got up and stalked to the bar, ordering a drink. But with the dire situation I'd found myself in, my resolve to have just one beer tonight disintegrated. At the last minute, I ordered an extra. I was going to need it to drown out the spark kindling into a goddamn wildfire with every passing minute. I dropped my head, staring down at the sticky countertop, and wished for the strength to get through this evening without saying, or worse, doing something I'd regret.

I had a lot of regrets over Nate Mathews. I didn't need to add to them.

When solid, thick forearms rested on the bar top beside me, I didn't even need to glance up to know who they belonged to. His scent hadn't changed. He still smelled of pine trees and fresh air, with the added tang of motor oil. I knew if I looked over, I'd find a smudge of it somewhere. Maybe on his forehead or his shirt. If he wasn't on the back of a bull, he was under a car or working on his motorcycle.

At least, he had been. Before he left.

I couldn't face him. My cheeks were already hot, and I didn't want to give Nate the satisfaction of making me blush.

"Hey, Hallie."

I groaned internally. His voice had changed since the last time I'd seen him. If it were even possible, it had somehow become deeper. More gravelly. Sexier. Damn him.

I tapped my fingers on the countertop, wishing Anthony would hurry the hell up with my beer. How long did it take to uncap a bottle and grab a few dollars from my hand?

Long enough for Nate to corner me, apparently.

He leaned in closer, and it was as if time crawled to a halt, his movements switching to slow motion. I saw what was coming before it happened. He was going to nudge me with his arm. Make contact with my skin. Touch me.

In my head, I yelped and moved away quick enough that no contact could be made.

In reality, my horny, traitorous body stood completely still and welcomed the touch of his arm against mine, even if it was covered by a T-shirt sleeve.

I closed my eyes for the tiniest second as that wildfire consumed me.

"Not gonna talk to me?" he asked casually, like it had only been yesterday that we'd been friends, not years ago. He had to be kidding if he thought I was going to talk to him after everything that had happened *that night*.

Anthony put the two beers on the countertop, but before I could even pick them up and hightail it back to the relative safety of my table, Nate snatched one.

"Hey!" I jerked in surprise and made the mistake of looking Nate in the face.

I immediately wished I hadn't. I took in every detail in the space of a second, my heart pounding. Dark blond stubble coated his strong jaw. The slight upturn of his lips, like he was pleased to see me. The hair that stuck out from beneath his tattered ball cap was longer than he'd worn it in high school, but the perfect length for grabbing if we were kissing...or doing other things.

I swallowed hard; shutting down that part of me that still wanted him. It was just my hormones. Nothing more. A physical reaction to a pretty face and a body made for sin.

He took a swig of *my* beer, eyeing me over the top of it. "Dance with me?"

Thank God I hadn't taken a sip because I would have spit it all over him. On second thought, that might not have been the worst thing in the world. Watching sticky beer saliva spray all over his too-handsome face would have been momentarily satisfying. He would have deserved it. Beer stealer.

Heartbreaker.

"I'd rather dance with Two Toe Tom than you."

Two Toe Tom was the local drunk and about a hundred years old, regularly found slumped at the end of the bar with his graying beard soaking in a glass of half-drunk bourbon. He'd lost most of his toes to frostbite one winter, when he'd gotten drunk and passed out during a once-in-a-hundred-year snowstorm that had ripped through the usually mild-weathered town. Or so the story went anyway.

Nate glanced in Tom's direction and shrugged. "Don't think he's up for it."

"And neither am I." I pushed away from the bar, with my solitary beer clutched firmly in my fingers.

"You can't go. I owe you a drink."

"You don't owe me anything, Nate. Not a damn thing." I spun on my heel and stalked back to Summer and Austin.

They both stared at me with big eyes.

"Brutal," Austin whispered.

Summer, awesome best friend that she was, jumped to my defense. "She has a right to be pissed."

"Thank you," I said, putting a fist out for her to bump.

She grinned at me as our knuckles touched. "But maybe you should talk to him? Clear the air? It's been four years..."

I pressed my fingers so hard into the bottle I was surprised it didn't shatter. "It could be fifty years. It still wouldn't be enough."

Summer nodded more firmly this time. "Right. Okay, if

that's how you want to play it, I'm completely on board and president of the We Hate Nate Club. I'll get T-shirts made and clear a spot on my bumper for a sticker."

I couldn't help but grin at that and relief tinged her eyes when she realized I wasn't really mad. We'd been best friends for four years now. Ever since Nate had left, she'd been my right-hand woman. I could never stay angry at her for more than a minute or two. Normally we didn't argue much at all, and this was definitely something I needed her to have my back on.

Nate could waltz back into town if he wanted to. He could sit across the bar and look handsome as hell. But there was no way I was forgiving him. Not in a million years.

2

NATE

Hallie fucking Ryan.

I'd promised myself that when I came back home, I wouldn't try to talk to her. Yet I'd dragged my sister, her husband, and their devil spawn daughter to the Black Bull, knowing Hallie would be there. Everybody was at the Black Bull on Friday nights. There was nowhere else to go in this tiny dead-end town. If you wanted a beer and a feed, you had no other options.

I'd known she'd be here, and I'd come because I couldn't stay away from her. It had been different when I was on tour. With millions of miles between us, it had been easier to lock the memories of Hallie up in a little box and tuck it into the back of mind. Even then, I never really forgot about her. Hallie was not the sort of woman any man could forget in a hurry. The other guys on tour gave me shit for not being interested in the women who threw themselves at us, but I just shook my head and said I had my reasons.

All my reasons started with H and ended in ALLIE. But what could I do, working all the way on the other side of

America? Or worse, Australia or Brazil. My job as a bull rider on the WBRA tour was a dream come true in every way. Except one. And I was staring right at her.

Shep, my sister's husband, chuckled as I slumped back into my seat and crossed my arms over my chest.

"Shut up," I griped at him.

He held his hands up in mock surrender, but his shit-eating grin of amusement was impossible to miss. "Just never thought I'd see the day where you'd actually try your luck with Hallie Ryan again."

I paused with the beer bottle halfway to my lips. "What does that mean?"

My sister, Jasmine, rolled her eyes, her little daughter bouncing up and down on her knees, cute as a button when it was her mama holding her. "After what you did to her on prom night? You've got nerves of steel."

I shot her a dirty look. "Does everybody in this backward-ass town know about that?"

"Not everyone."

The laughter in Shep's eyes was telling. "Just most."

I groaned and focused back on Jasmine. "You're a woman. Scale of one to ten. How badly did I fuck up?"

She cocked her head to one side, considering my question. "One being not at all, ten being colossal mistake that should have made world news?"

I nodded. "Sure. Whatever."

"About a seventy."

"Seventy!"

She shrugged. "You have no idea what it's like to be a seventeen-year-old girl on prom night if you think you're getting out of this one easily. And then to compound it, you left."

I scraped my hand through my hair. This was worse

than I thought. I sipped at my beer again but then put it back on the table. Damn it. I knew coming back here and trying to fix things with Hallie wasn't going to be simple, but I only had a week. I'd expected to have to grovel for a night, but then I thought we could have spent the rest of the week doing all the things we'd never gotten to do as teenagers.

Apparently, I was wrong. Shit. Stealing her beer probably hadn't helped any either. What the hell had I been thinking?

"I asked her to dance. She said no. Should I ask again?"

Jasmine gaped at me like I'd grown an extra head. "Have the bull shit—" She grimaced and shot an apologetic glance at her husband. "Sorry, I know we're not swearing around Molly."

He gave her a tolerant smile.

I rolled my eyes at that. They'd turned into such...*parents* since I'd been gone.

Jasmine swiveled back to continue berating me. "What I was saying was, have the bull *poo* fumes gone to your brain? You don't ask her to dance if she already said no. You're jumping the gun entirely. You need to get her attention first. But from a distance. Give the woman some space."

I didn't like the sound of space. Not when all I wanted to do was get closer to her. The last night I'd seen her she'd been in a fancy dress that swept the floor. She'd looked like some fairy-tale princess. But I liked the way she looked tonight better. With her long blonde hair swept up into a high ponytail, loose tendrils falling around her face. Her jeans molded to her ass and hips. And those lips...she was completely free of makeup, but those lips drew my eye from across the room. Full and pink, and all I could think about was how they'd feel beneath my own.

Jasmine obviously knew women better than I did. And

my lame attempt at winning Hallie over just now had resulted in her ignoring me, then dismissing me outright, so I obviously needed some help.

Molly, my niece, rubbed at her eyes with her fists, and let out a whine of complaint.

Jasmine held her out to me.

I pushed my chair backward. "Whoa, what are you doing? You know that kid hates me."

"She doesn't hate you. She just doesn't know you. Take your niece."

"But why?" I liked babies. At least I thought I did. But I'd had absolutely nothing to do with them. I'd held Molly a few times in the last couple of days since I'd come back to stay with my sister, but it hadn't gone down well. She'd taken one look at me and held her chubby arms out for one of her parents to rescue her. A few times that had been accompanied by wailing. Right now, she appeared ready to launch into a full-scale tantrum at the prospect of me taking her.

"Do you want to win Hallie over or not? You know what women love?" She thrust Molly into my arms, forcing me to cradle her small body to my chest or drop her.

"They love a man with a baby. If Hallie won't dance with you, go dance with your niece. It'll work. Guarantee it."

I shot a glance at the mostly empty dance floor, then shook my head at my sister. "I'm not doing that!"

She shrugged and held a hand out to her husband. "Fine. But Molly is exhausted, and the quickest way to get her to sleep is to get up and sway. We're going to dance, so you're on your own, little brother."

I looked to Shep in dismay, but he just winked at me and wrapped an arm around his wife. The two of them threaded their way through the tables and found themselves a spot in the middle of the dance floor. I wrinkled my nose at the two of them. Shep gazed down at Jasmine like she was the sun and the moon.

It was sickening how in love they were. But I didn't miss the pang of jealousy that echoed around my chest either. It only reminded me how far away I was from having something like that, and how different my life might have been if I'd stayed here after prom, instead of running away to ride bulls.

Molly squawked, and I patted her on the back awkwardly. "Shh, baby girl. Go to sleep."

Molly wasn't having any of it. She fidgeted and flailed in my arms, throwing herself around, her tired cries growing louder.

I couldn't blame Jasmine for wanting a moment with her husband. I was her only family, and Shep's parents lived in Australia. I knew the two of them hadn't had a minute alone since Molly's arrival eight months ago. That was on me because I never came home.

I pushed to my feet. "Okay, looks like we're dancing, too."

I stood, and with the rhythm of the slow country song, I swayed from side to side. I wasn't a dancer by any stretch of the imagination. But even I could manage a side-to-side shuffle on the beat.

Instantly, Molly laid her velvety soft head down on my shoulder, her cries and fussing quieting. She stopped rubbing her eyes and found her thumb to suck instead.

"Thank fuck," I muttered. Then realized I'd cussed. "Oops. Don't tell your mama I said that." On instinct, I tilted my head so my cheek rested against Molly's wispy hair. God, she was so soft and sweet. At least when she was sleeping. I'd missed all of this while I'd been away. I'd missed seeing her as a tiny baby. I'd missed getting to watch my sister and Shep try to work out what to do with a newborn.

I dared a glance in Hallie's direction.

She was watching, and this time as our gazes met, she didn't immediately turn away. Something flashed across her face, but it was gone before I could really comprehend what it was.

I spun Molly around, so Hallie wouldn't see my grin. Perhaps Jasmine had been right after all. I shuffled out onto the dance floor, where nobody in the bar could miss me. Another little glance at Hallie told me I had her attention. "Thanks for being cuter than me," I whispered to Molly. "It's working like a charm."

The words died in my throat as one of the cowboys, at the table next to Hallie's, stood and held a hand out to her. She nodded, putting her fingers through his. He led her to the dance floor, stopping just a foot or two away from where I stood.

The cowboy nodded at me. "Cute baby."

"Thanks," I fumbled. But it was Hallie I couldn't stop staring at.

Her dance partner didn't seem to notice. He pulled her into his arms, keeping a respectful distance between them, despite the slow beat of the romantic country song. Hallie shot a look at me, then closed the gap between them, wrapping her arms around his neck and smiling up at him.

If I'd been jealous watching Jasmine and Shep, I didn't have a name for the feeling I had now, watching some other guy hold Hallie like that. Sure, I knew that it had been years since the two of us had danced at prom. I logically knew she would have had boyfriends. Or one-night stands. Both probably. She was no wallflower. She wasn't sitting around, waiting for me to come home. But that had been easier to think about when it wasn't right there in my face.

Shit. I had no idea what I was thinking, coming back here, hoping I could just walk into her life like I'd never left. The realization hit me like a ton of bricks.

I'd spent all this time pining over a woman who either still hated me or just didn't care anymore.

Jasmine gazed at me with sad eyes as I passed the sleeping baby back to her.

"Nate..."

I smiled and shook my head. "No, it's fine. It's all good. I think I'm going to go home."

"We'll come, too. Molly needs to go to bed anyway."

I smiled tightly, avoiding turning in Hallie's direction, and feeling even worse that Jasmine and Shep were cutting their evening short because of me. Not wanting to make a scene by arguing, I tried to be helpful, grabbing Molly's baby bag from the table we'd been sitting at and shoved the strap up on my shoulder.

I could feel the weight of someone's gaze on me, but I didn't dare turn around to see if it was Hallie's. If I was wrong, and she was actually making out with that cowboy, I'd be in all sorts of trouble. Instead, I slipped out the bar door without a look back.

Outside, a full moon shined, the only real source of light. The parking lot was nothing more than a dirt yard, and the streetlights were farther away. I trudged to Shep's four-wheel drive to put the baby bag in the back, feeling foolish.

I'd brought my bike instead of traveling into town with my sister and brother-in-law. I'd told my sister it was because I might want to stay on if she left early with the baby.

I realized now I'd subconsciously been hoping to leave

with Hallie. There was this place I loved, down by the river. A romantic make-out spot.

Foolish.

Shep clapped a hand over my shoulder in a fatherly sort of way. He was only about five years older than I was, but his life was light-years from mine. He worked his ass off, day in and day out, on the ranch my sister and I had inherited when our parents had passed away years ago. I worked hard, too, but in an entirely different way. My job was full of fitness training in hotel gyms, press conferences, and Saturday night rodeos with my name in lights. When the World Bull Riding Association had come knocking after I turned eighteen, I'd jumped at the chance. I wasn't sure I was cut out for the rural sort of lifestyle my sister had. I wanted to travel. I'd wanted to see the world.

That's what I'd done. I'd left my sister and Shep behind.

And Hallie, too.

I swung my leg over my bike and gunned the engine. I only had a few more days here anyway. With a low rev of my engine, I slowly followed after Shep and Jasmine, heading toward the driveway that would lead us out onto the main road.

I waited behind while they stopped to check the road was clear, but all I could think of was Hallie, and how that might be the last time I saw her. Who knew when I'd be back next? Hell, if I came back in a few years, she could be married with a family. Or she might have moved on from this town entirely.

The thought didn't sit well with me.

I was so preoccupied I barely even noticed Shep pull out onto the road.

I almost didn't notice the truck coming in the other direction, with both headlights off.

Neither did Shep.

All I definitely noticed was the explosion of sound the two vehicles made as they collided, and the sickening crunch of metal against metal.

Shep's car, with my entire family inside, flipped and rolled off the road.

3

HALLIE

Over Jason's shoulder, I watched Nate leave the bar with his family and felt like a bitch. I knew what I'd done. I'd accepted the dance with Jason and made it out to be more than it truly was, in the hopes of making Nate jealous.

The fact it had worked was the real surprise. Sort of. It had been hurt that had flashed in Nate's eyes, not jealousy. Yet he hadn't said a word. He'd just quietly handed his sister back her baby, and he'd left the bar.

I was the worst sort of pond scum.

We'd been best friends our whole lives, and I couldn't even talk to the guy when he came back to town after four years away?

"Dammit," I whispered.

Jason pulled back. "You okay?"

Jason's concern was worse. He was a nice guy, and we were friends, but nothing more. "Yeah, fine. I'm sorry about this..." I gestured between us. "It's a bit much."

He lifted one shoulder. "We're just dancing."

I was glad he saw it that way. I didn't want to feel like I'd been using him. But I couldn't stand by while Nate walked out of my life again. Not without hashing out what had happened between us. "I gotta go," I told Jason. "Can you let Summer know?"

He gave me a knowing smile. "Sure. See you at the ranch on Monday."

I ran for the bar door and shoved it open. "Nate!" I scanned the parking lot, my heart sinking when I didn't see him anywhere. But then a flash of taillights caught my attention at the far end of the lot. I raised a hand, waving frantically at Nate on the back of his bike, stopped behind his sister's four-wheel drive. Yelling was useless, but I tried again anyway, because, dammit, now that I'd decided this confrontation needed to happen, I needed it to happen now. I'd lose my courage if I had to wait until the next time I saw him.

I ran for Nate's bike, right as Shep pulled out onto the road.

No amount of watching high-speed collisions on the news or YouTube prepared you to see or hear something like that. The impact of the truck hitting Shep's SUV was shockingly violent. I flinched away, covering my head and eyes on instinct, but that didn't block out the noise as the car flipped and rolled, sliding off the edge of the road and down into the embankment. The impact was deafening, ringing in my ears, and instantly the smell of burnt rubber and gasoline permeated the air.

However, it was the deadly silence that settled in the aftermath that filled me with fear. That silence was somehow worse than watching the crash itself.

But it was the pause my body needed to come back to

life. I ran for the overturned car, barely visible on the other side of the road. I passed Nate's bike, abandoned on the driveway, no sign of its owner anywhere. The gravel road and broken glass crunched beneath my boots. I skidded across it, half falling down the hill on the other side, only just catching myself on the patchy grass with my hands.

I clapped a hand over my mouth. "Oh my God."

The four-wheel drive was crumpled from every angle and lying on its roof. Tiny screams from the baby inside pierced the air, sickening me to my core.

At least she was alive. There wasn't a sound from either of her parents, and that scared me more.

Nate's yell of frustration and fear sent me skittering to his side. He blinked up at me from the ground, confusion and surprise in his eyes, but we didn't have time for that.

Everything that had passed between us didn't matter anymore.

"I called the ambulance, but I can't get the doors open," he said frantically. "I'm too big to get through the windows."

I dropped to the ground as he stood to get out of my way. Lying on my stomach, I peered into the mangled wreck of the car through the rear window. The glass had busted out, but the metal frame on this side remained mostly in shape.

In the front seat, Jasmine's head hung limply, her blood glistening in the dim glow of the dashboard lights. I couldn't see Shep's face. His seat belt hadn't held him in place as well as Jasmine's, and he was slumped in an unnatural position, his neck twisted awkwardly.

Terror whispered he might already be dead.

I pushed the thought away, because I instinctively knew there was nothing I could do to help either of them. But I could help their daughter. Safe in her baby seat, Molly screamed her lungs out, her legs and arms wiggling in the air. She was the sort of baby who smiled at everyone she passed in the street. The delight of the whole town. But right now, her face was red with the exertion of her terrified cries.

I inched forward, trying not to choke on the overwhelming smell. Liquid seeped into the body of the car and pooled beneath me. "Hey, sweetheart. It's okay." I reached for her, but Nate was right, the gap was tiny and the car was big enough that I couldn't easily reach her with one hand. I wriggled in a few more inches until a hand clamped on my leg.

"Hallie! There's gas leaking everywhere!"

I looked back at Nate, crouching behind me. I knew what he wasn't saying.

This thing could go up at any minute.

It didn't matter. Not when I knew I could get to Molly and get her out. "I know. Let go."

He stared at me for a moment, then reluctantly did as I said.

I fought my way through the gap, trying to reach Molly's seat belt, scraping myself on the shards of broken glass. They pierced my skin, opening it up until blood trickled across my arms and shoulders and abdomen, but I refused to stop. I wouldn't be the one who gave up on this little girl and left her for dead. If the car went up in flames right now, I'd go with it. Blood pounded in my ears at that realization, the rushing noise urging me on.

I didn't feel the pain of the injuries I was inflicting on myself. The seconds felt like hours as I slithered across the debris, but then I was finally close enough to untangle her from the straps, catching her awkwardly as her body slipped from them. Her screams started up in earnest again, filling me with dread that I might have just hurt her more. "Shhh, it's okay, I've got you." I tucked her downy head to my chest and backed out of the crumpled car as quickly as I could.

In the time I'd been inside the car, the guys from the bar had filtered out to help. Three of them yanked at the passenger-side door, trying to pry it from its hinges.

Nate looked up from working to free his sister. Relief flickered across his expression, but then it morphed into something harder. "Get her out of here!"

He was right. I knew that. I had to get Molly away from the car that could explode at any minute.

But I hated leaving Nate.

It suddenly felt like I was being ripped in two.

Nate had no such qualms. "Dammit, Hallie. Go!"

I turned and ran, clutching Molly to my chest. Summer met me halfway down the embankment, and it was only then that I realized the rest of the bar patrons had all come outside and were standing at the edge of the road, watching the scene unfold in horror.

Summer held her arms out. "Here, give her to me."

But I couldn't. Some protective instinct in me had me holding Molly even tighter. "No, we're fine."

Summer frowned but didn't push. She wrapped an arm around me and helped pull me up the rest of the embankment to where Austin was waiting.

"You shouldn't have gone down there!" he scolded Summer. "You could have been killed!"

I just stared at him. What the actual fuck? She'd been about three steps down the hill, not inside the damn car like I had been. Like Nate still was.

"My best friend was down there!" she yelled at him. "People are hurt."

I turned away from them, straining my eyes in the darkness, trying to work out if Molly was injured while also keeping an eye on her uncle.

A rescue truck screamed onto the scene, sirens blaring, four guys in uniform pouring from the inside and shouldering their equipment. One took charge, his voice booming out over the surrounding noise. "Everybody get back!"

Nate wouldn't listen. He had to be dragged up to the road in order to let them work. But only the tiniest part of me was relieved that he was out of the danger zone. The guys from the bar held him, but he fought with them the entire time, his whole focus on getting to his sister and brother-in-law.

"Nate!" I snapped at him, feeling harsh for speaking to him in that tone, but this wasn't the time for kind, soft words. "Stop. You can't do anything for your sister right now. But you can for Molly."

He stilled, swiveling in my direction and blinking at me as if he'd forgotten we were here. "Is she okay?" he choked out. He reached out a hand to me but dropped it before he could make contact. "Are you? You're bleeding."

"I'll be fine. Do you want to take her?"

He held his hands out for his niece, but his fingers trembled so hard he bunched them into fists, dropping them at his sides. "Fuck!" He shook his head, his gaze slipping back down the embankment to where the rescue workers had the Jaws of Life out, cutting into the car. "I can't. I'll drop her. Or hurt her."

He was in shock, I realized, and probably needed medical attention himself.

He didn't need the pressure of caring for Molly as well.

I squeezed his forearm. "It's okay. I got her."

Blue and red lights lit up his face momentarily, and I glanced over my shoulder at three ambulances pulling up at the scene. Summer ran across the road to grab the nearest one and hauled the woman in my direction.

I squeezed Nate's arm again. "I'll stay with her, okay? You just worry about Shep and Jasmine."

His eyes were wild and unfocused. "Thank you."

I went with Summer and let one paramedic take Molly from me, while the other sat me on the opposite side of the ambulance to inspect my injuries.

"You're going to need some stitches," the woman said to me, wincing in sympathy. She handed me some gauze for a wound on my arm.

"What about Molly? Is she okay? Just worry about her. I'm fine."

The paramedic frowned at me, but she checked with her partner.

She nodded. "Somehow she seems to have avoided any noticeable injuries at all. But we still need to get her to the hospital for a full range of checks and scans."

Molly was screaming again, and the sound ripped at my heart. "Can I hold her? Just until we get to the hospital?"

The two women nodded, handing her back to me before clambering out of the ambulance. Molly immediately quieted, and I hugged the tiny girl to my chest.

Summer watched from the back of the ambulance, her brown eyes huge. "What can I do? Should I come?" she asked, as the paramedics readied to close the doors.

Fear and pain trickled through the adrenaline. I would have loved to have my best friend climb in beside me. But then I thought about Nate being at the scene by himself. He and Summer had trained together at Summer's dad's bull riding school. We'd all gone to school together. She knew him almost as well as I did, and he could use her help and support more than I could right now. "Stay. Make sure someone looks at him, too, okay?"

"Of course. I'll meet you up at the hospital as soon as they get Shep and Jasmine out."

I prayed they'd both be alive when that happened.

4

NATE

The crash played over and over again in my head. No matter how many times I blinked to try to force it away, it kept coming back, determined to haunt me. The images brought the whispers of guilt with them, and pacing the halls of the hospital didn't help any.

Shep and Jasmine wouldn't have even been at the bar that night if I hadn't dragged them there. They wouldn't have been leaving at that time if I hadn't gotten butthurt over Hallie's rejection. If I hadn't come back to town, they would have spent their Friday night sitting on their couch watching *Friends* reruns, instead of lying in hospital beds, fighting for their lives.

The doctor came out, folding his arms across his chest. "Nate, right? Jasmine's brother? She talks about you a lot."

I held my hand out for my sister's colleague to shake. I'd momentarily forgotten she worked here at the hospital. Or at least she had, before Molly. Had she returned from maternity leave yet? Hell, what kind of brother was I, that I didn't even know the answer to that?

One who was never around.

"Yes, I'm her brother. Is she okay? What about Shep? I mean, Lachlan Shepherd. He's my brother-in-law. I called his parents, but they're overseas and can't get here until..." I was rambling with nerves, telling the doctor things he didn't need to know but I couldn't seem to stop myself.

Thankfully, the man took pity on me. Or maybe he was just used to this sort of barely coherent response from the family of his patients.

"Jasmine and Shep are both doing as well as can be expected."

"They're alive?" I breathed out the words I hadn't dared to say out loud. Because neither of them had looked good when they'd finally been pulled from the wreckage. I hadn't been allowed in the ambulance with them, but Summer had driven me, insisting I wasn't driving myself. Shit, I didn't even know where my bike was. I'd abandoned it to the road the moment I'd seen that truck hit Shep's car. Had the truck driver even stopped?

The doctor smiled at me. "They're very much alive. And we're going to keep them that way. But I need you to prepare yourself. Neither of them will have a quick recovery. It's going to be long, and probably painful."

"They're tough," I said with conviction. You had to be when you worked the land. Shep might have been the one doing most of the heavy lifting at the ranch lately, but Jasmine had grown up right beside me. She knew how to brand a calf, put in a fence, or fix a tractor with the best of them. She had calloused hands, like everybody else in this town. She'd fight. I knew she would. She had to, for Molly.

"Shit, Molly. Hallie." I whirled around as if they'd just appear out of nowhere, then I realized that was ridiculous. "Do you know where they are? Jasmine's daughter and..." Hell, how did I describe Hallie? I had no words. I never had.

"The woman she came in with. I think she might have been injured." *Fuck!* How had I let Molly and Hallie go by themselves? What kind of uncle—hell, what kind of man—did that? I should have been with them the entire time.

The doctor checked an iPad and pointed me in the direction of the pediatric ward. With the knowledge that my sister was going to be okay, I ran for the elevator, but when the ancient thing didn't open instantly, I slammed my way through the doorway of the emergency stairwell and raced up the two flights of stairs. My gaze darted from room number to room number, mentally figuring out which direction room 307 would be, before taking off down the hall again.

A nurse in green scrubs gave me the side-eye as I ran past, but nobody stopped me. I skidded to a halt in the doorway, peering through the small glass peephole window.

I couldn't name the emotion that welled inside, but it spread through me like molasses, slowing my heart rate and calming my erratic breathing. I pushed the door open, quiet and controlled, and the complete opposite to the chaos of the last few hours.

Molly was tucked into a bed much too big for her, with the white metal rails raised to keep her from falling out. She had a single monitor attached to her by a cord, but she slept soundly, no trace of the trauma she'd suffered on her little face.

Slumped uncomfortably in a hospital chair, Hallie slept with her arm through the railing, her fingers around Molly's. But unlike the baby, Hallie's face was lined with worry, even in her sleep. Another flash of guilt gnawed at me. I'd lumped all of this on her, so lost in my fear I hadn't even stopped to consider the strain I'd put her under.

This wasn't her problem. None of it was. I'd just gone

straight back to relying on her the way I always had as kids. What gave me the right to do that? We hadn't spoken in years.

A tremor ran through her body, so I grabbed a spare blanket from a pile sitting on a shelf and went to put it over her. I paused, noticing how ripped and torn her shirt was. And not only that, it was covered in patches of dried blood.

Hallie blinked her eyes open, then jolted half out of her chair when she saw me standing over her. Her fingers jerked from Molly's grasp, and the baby made a noise of annoyance in her sleep but quickly settled again.

Hallie pushed to her feet so we were closer to the same height. "What are you doing?" she hissed.

I held the blanket up as if that explained everything, but when she didn't respond, I realized she wasn't a mind reader. "You're cold. I was going to cover you up."

She jerked back an inch. "Oh. That's...nice."

"But then I saw you were covered in blood."

She gazed down at herself and grimaced. "It's fine."

"It's not. Did the nurses even clean those cuts? They're going to get infected."

She shrugged, peering down at Molly again. "I let them stitch the worst of them, and they brought some things to clean out the rest..." She pointed to a little green surgical bowl that held tweezers and gauze and antiseptic. "But Molly was crying, and I wanted to be the one to give her a bottle." She looked at me sheepishly. "I know I don't really know her. But I've met her a couple of times when I've run into Jasmine at the store. And I got her out of the car...I just felt like I was a bit more familiar than a random nurse, even though they're lovely."

I stared at her in amazement. She'd refused medical

treatment she obviously needed, just to take care of Molly. "I should have been here to do that," I mumbled.

Hallie bit her lip, not saying anything. Nothing needed to be said. We both knew I was right.

Hallie shifted toward the door. "I guess I should go, now that you're here."

"No," I said, before I could really think about it.

She stopped and tilted her head at me, like I'd confused her. Hell, I'd confused myself. The woman had been up all night with a baby who wasn't hers, because I hadn't been able to get my shit together. Of course she wanted to leave.

But I wasn't ready for her to walk out of my life again. Especially not with injuries that had at least partially been my fault. I glanced around, gaze landing on the antiseptic the nurses had brought to dress her wounds. "Can I clean your cuts?" I asked politely, as if we were complete strangers.

She frowned. "Do you know how?"

"Do you even know how many times I've come off a bull? Or my bike? Trust me, I know how to get out glass and gravel and clean a wound. Sit." I pointed at the chair before she could try to leave again.

She saluted me. "Being on tour has made you bossy."

I didn't tell her I was still the easy-going guy I'd been when we knew each other, and that it was just her and the desire to make sure she was okay that had me ordering her around. She'd sat, so that was all I really needed.

"Dammit, Hallie," I murmured, touching the collar of her shirt, surveying the damage. "Can I take this off you?"

She snorted on a laugh but waved her hand around. "Sure. It's pretty much rags now anyway."

"What are you laughing at?"

She shrugged. "It's just those are the words I thought you'd be saying a few years ago."

Shit. She'd gone there.

I cleared my throat. "You didn't give me the chance. You were already pretty naked by the time I got there."

She groaned. "You know what, do we have to do this right now? I'm tired and sore, and you don't need this. I'm sorry I brought it up."

I sighed. "No, I guess not. But I do need to clean these cuts." I slid the shirt off her shoulders and down her arms. I didn't miss the tremble that rolled down her spine as my fingertips brushed across the back of her neck and I tucked that away for future reference.

Hallie Ryan might not want to talk about our past, but she deserved to know the truth.

I wanted a second chance.

And I wasn't leaving this town until I'd explained everything.

5

NATE

Molly's doctor gave her the all clear to go home on Saturday afternoon, releasing her into my care. I was exhausted after being awake for over twenty-four hours, but then the doctor told me Jasmine was asking for me, so I ran down to her room like a bat out of Hell. Molly griped at me the entire way, completely unimpressed that I was not her mom or dad.

I burst into Jasmine's room without knocking. Her head turned stiffly in my direction, and when she noticed Molly, she burst into tears, holding her arms out for her daughter.

I leaned in so they could touch, but I wasn't sure Jasmine was actually strong enough to hold her, so I didn't dare let her go. My assumption proved correct, Jasmine's arms dropping back to the bed. "Just sit her on the bed by me. Please. I was so worried."

"She's fine," I assured my sister. "Hallie got her out and stayed with her until I could take over. She was amazing. How are you?"

It was a stupid question. Her head was bandaged, one

leg was in a foot-to-thigh cast, and she'd had surgery to repair a tear in her abdomen.

"I've been better." She tried to smile, but it was forced. "Shep still isn't awake."

The agony in her expression drove a needle in my heart. She was my sister, and even though she was older, I still had the urge to protect her. But I couldn't. Not from this sort of pain.

I grabbed her hand and squeezed it. "He'll wake up. His body just needs a little more rest." I tried to sound as confident as possible, but I knew it was falling on deaf ears. There was nothing I could say or do to reassure her that her husband would wake up and be the same man he'd been when we'd left the bar last night. No one could guarantee her that. All I could do was try to ease any other concerns she might have. I didn't need to be a parent to know Molly was her number two worry, right after her dad. "I've got this," I assured my sister. "Molly, I mean."

Jasmine lifted a hand limply, trying to wave it at me. "You can't. You need to go back on tour. Shep's parents—"

"Are in Australia. They're trying to get here, but it will be a few days. Shep's dad had some sort of business thing ..."

Worry flickered in my sister's eyes. "You've got to go back on tour in a few days."

"I'll postpone."

"You'll get fired."

She had a point, but there was nothing I could do about that right now.

I didn't want her panicking about me. "We'll work something out. You should sleep now."

She simply closed her eyes, too tired to even agree with me. But when I went to pull away, she grabbed my hand. "Nate?"

"Yeah?"

Her voice was barely more than a whisper, and she hadn't even opened her eyes. "Fix things with Hallie. Tell her how you feel. It could have been you last night...If you'd pulled out first, on your bike...and then she never would have known."

I couldn't argue with her. I couldn't make her understand it wasn't just as easy as all that. I'd apologized a million times after I'd left. I'd called Hallie night and day, begging her for a chance to explain.

She hadn't wanted to hear it.

Molly and I left Jasmine to sleep and took the elevator down to the ground floor exit. That was as far as I got before I realized I had absolutely no way of getting back to Shep and Jasmine's place. There was no Uber in this town. No taxis. There was a bus than ran every three hours but had finished the last run of the day. "Shit," I said to Molly, then cringed. "I mean, shoot. I'm not supposed to be swearing in front of you, am I?"

Her answering gurgle wasn't much help, but I knew it was what my sister wanted. Not swearing in front of their child was the least I could do while I was in charge of her.

Well, that, and keeping her alive.

I wasn't entirely sure I was capable of either. And the fact I was stranded in town meant we weren't off to the greatest of starts.

"I went to school in this town, how is it that I don't have a single friend to call?"

That wasn't really true. I'd had a couple of male friends, but I didn't even have their numbers anymore. I just hadn't cared to keep in touch once we'd left school. Which showed how close we'd been, that we could all walk away so easily.

Hallie was my one true friend. The one I'd called on for everything.

Shit. Argh, shoot. Whatever. I couldn't call her again. She'd only left the hospital a few hours ago and was probably asleep.

Molly let out a squawk of disapproval at waiting around so long, so I jostled her and the bag of bottles and formula samples the hospital had given me into one arm. Then I dug through my pocket for my phone and called Summer.

6

HALLIE

The front door opened and closed, and I paused with my fingers gripped around the moldy old carpet I was ripping up. "What's the password?" I yelled down the stairs.

"Daisy?" Summer called back, amongst the shuffle of dumping her purse on the floor by the door. "Like the one on your ass?"

"Wrong. But you can come up anyway. I guess I know you, since you know about my tattoo."

Her footsteps pounded up the stairs, and she poked her head around the corner. "I need a password now?"

"Just wanted to be sure I wasn't being robbed. That's the last thing I need."

Summer wrinkled her nose in the direction of the stinking carpet. "No offense, babe, but ain't nobody going to be robbing you anytime soon. There's nothing here to steal. Apart from flaking wallpaper and maybe asbestos."

I sighed. "I know. This place is a dump. But it has good bones. It'll be amazing once I'm done with it."

Summer rolled up the sleeves on her denim shirt and

pushed them up over her elbows. "It's going to be the best bed and breakfast in miles. You're going to put us on the map."

"I think you and your dad already did that with your bull riding school."

Summer's dad, Kai 'Frost' Hunt, had been a champion bull rider in his twenties and thirties. And he'd been training champions ever since. They ran a boarding program, taking in cowboys from all over the country who wanted to train under Kai's watchful eye. But Summer was no slouch herself. She was her dad's protégé and headed for the big time.

"What are you doing here anyway? Shouldn't you be training? The rodeo at Masonville is next weekend. You need the points to stay in contention for the WBRA, right?"

Summer pulled at the edge of another section of carpet that had to be removed. "Yeah, but Dad won't let me. He thinks I've been training too hard."

I raised an eyebrow at that. "Is there such a thing when you're training for the pros?"

"That's what I said! But he thinks he knows best."

I side-eyed her. "He did win the WBRA title about ten times."

"Three times. Like that makes him some sort of expert." She grinned, and we both burst into laughter. Summer and her dad were thick as thieves, and the whole town knew he was her hero. She'd been riding bulls her entire life, just trying to walk in his footsteps. And she was going to do it, too.

"I can't wait to watch you qualify for the tour. 'Bout time a woman made it on to the team and showed all those guys what's what." I tossed my rolled-up bit of gross carpet out the second-story window and down into the pile I was creating outside. A cloud of dust rose, and I shut the window before any of it could come back inside the house. Renovating a hundred-year-old property that hadn't been updated since the sixties was not for the faint of heart. This work was dirty and gross. But I'd never shied away from it. This house was my dream, and I was damn determined to make it a reality. It just sucked Summer wouldn't be here to see it.

I pouted in her direction. "I'm going to miss you when you're gone. Stupid WBRA. Taking all my people."

"Nate's your person now?"

I shrugged. "No. But he was. You two are gonna go off and have a ball seeing the world, while I'm here YouTubing do-it-yourself tiling techniques because I'm too damn broke to pay someone to do this work for me."

Summer tossed a grubby bit of underlay at me. "Stop it. You love this shit. Your idea of a good time is eating Cheetos while watching a home reno show."

Couldn't argue with her there. "I know. And I really am excited for you. You're going to be a superstar. Remind me to get your autograph before you leave. You know, for when you're so famous you forget my name, and just pass me in the streets like we never knew each other." I laughed because Summer was the most down-to-earth woman I'd ever met, and the thought of her success going to her head was ludicrous.

But I'd once thought that about Nate. And look how that had turned out.

"I wish Austin were happy for me. He never comes right out and says it, but he drops enough hints that tell me he's not pleased about the prospect of me going on tour."

I pressed my lips together and turned away.

Summer's sigh was loud. "Say it, Hal. I know you want to."

Well, if she insisted. "Austin just wants you barefoot and pregnant. He hates that your dreams are bigger than his. For the five millionth time, what on earth are you still doing with him? You're the most mismatched couple in the history of forever and—"

Her phone rang, and she rushed to pick it up.

"Saved by the bell," I muttered. "We aren't done with this conversation." But it was one I knew I wouldn't win, because we'd had it a dozen times before. It was no secret Summer's boyfriend and I weren't exactly friends. I might have teased her about leaving me, but she knew I was nothing but excited and proud of her.

I couldn't say the same for Austin.

"Nate? What's up?"

That got my attention. I widened my eyes in Summer's direction and mouthed, *My Nate?*

Not that he was my Nate anymore. He hadn't been mine for a long time, and one night of helping out during a traumatic event didn't change that.

She nodded.

Loud speaker, I mimed, and she hit the button on her phone.

Nate's voice filled the little room. "—stuck at the hospital with Molly and I have no way of getting back to Shep and Jasmine's house. I know it's a big ask, but is there any way you could come get us?"

"I'll come," I blurted out before Summer could answer.

She raised an eyebrow at me, and I clapped a hand over my mouth, just as surprised as she was.

"Hallie?"

I pried my fingers away from my face, a blush heating

my cheeks. "Hey, yeah. It's me. Summer has...things to do. But I can come. Be there in ten."

"Uh, okay. Thank you. That would be great."

I stabbed the red 'cancel call' button before he could even say goodbye, then turned to Summer with huge eyes. "What the hell was that?"

She laughed and put away her phone. "I've no idea. But get on your bike, sister. You've got a man and baby to collect."

7

HALLIE

Nerves thrummed through me as I drove myself downtown, headed for the hospital. It was one thing to be around Nate, full of adrenaline and preoccupied by whether or not his family was going to make it through the night. But now there was no adrenaline urging me on. Just nerves telling me I should turn around and go back home, because being in an enclosed space with Nate Mathews was not a good idea. It was only the thought of him trying to walk the thirty miles home with a baby on his hip that stopped me. Molly didn't need that, even if Nate deserved the blisters.

He was bouncing a cranky baby on his knee when I pulled up, and seemed distinctly relieved to see me, judging by the way the tension fell from his rigid shoulders. But he buried that quickly and grabbed his things, hauling them around to the passenger side and sliding in.

Molly gave me a gummy grin from his lap, and I smiled at her, patting her chubby cheek. But I couldn't stare at the baby all day. I had to force myself to look up into Nate's face at some point, and I may as well get it over and done with. I raised my gaze.

Nate smirked.

On one hand, I was sort of relieved. There'd been no smirking at the hospital earlier. All he'd had room for was worry and fear. This was more the Nate I knew. The one who'd spent our entire childhood and teenage years teasing me.

"What?" I asked him.

"You're still driving this piece-of-shit car?"

I slapped him across the biceps, then snapped my hand back like I'd been electrocuted. Whoa. That had been a very solid arm I'd just slapped. My gaze wandered to his shirt, noticing for the first time that his chest and shoulders filled it out so much better than they had the last time I'd seen him. But that was beside the point. He was dissing my car, and that couldn't go unchecked. "Rylee is a reliable old girl, and she says 'fuck you.'" I smiled sweetly at him.

To my surprise, there was no witty retort. Instead, he clapped his hands over Molly's ears. "You can't say *fuck* around her!"

I laughed. "What? She's like, six months old, Nate. She doesn't know fuck from buck."

He sighed. "She's eight months. Jasmine and Shep don't swear around her, so I'm just trying to do the right thing by them."

I softened a little at that, even though I still thought it was ridiculous. "Fine. Rylee says, '*buck* you' then."

He nodded, seemingly satisfied with that. I snorted on a laugh but covered it by revving the engine and pulling away from the hospital. I got us on the road out to the house Nate had grown up in. I knew it well, having ridden my bike from my parents' place out to his house many a time. We bumped over the roads in silence, Nate gripping Molly so hard she squirmed.

"Ease up a bit," I suggested. "She's not coated in Vaseline. You aren't going to drop her."

"Maybe not, but she should be in a car seat. I'm going to need to get one. This isn't safe."

He was right, but it was the best we could do on short notice. I sure as hell didn't have a baby seat just lying around my house. I didn't even know anyone with a baby, other than Shep and Jasmine.

I decided to distract him instead before he squeezed poor Molly into mush. "What's in the bag?"

Nate nudged the plastic bag at his feet. "Jasmine was still breastfeeding, so the hospital gave me some bottles and a bunch of different formula samples to try her with."

"She liked the one I gave her."

"Do you know what type that was?"

I shrugged. "No idea. The nurses made it up."

He sighed. "I haven't fed her yet. The nurses were eager to help, so I let them. I don't even know how hot to make her bottles."

He seemed so worried, I patted his shoulder, trying to be reassuring. But I think I only succeeded in reminding myself how good his arms looked now.

By the time I made it to Nate's street, Molly's squirming had become thrashing, accompanied by a wail of annoyance. Or hunger. Who knew? I didn't know much about babies either, though they didn't terrify me like they seemed to do with Nate.

Nate turned Molly around so she could see him, but that only made her cry harder. "Hey, shh, kiddo. It's okay. We're nearly there."

The moment I parked by the door, he got out, fumbling

with his belongings. “Uh, thanks Hallie. Really, thank you. You saved my skin.” He jogged for the front door, dropping his bag of supplies for Molly as he tried to get the door open at the same time. The bottles rolled all through the dirt, and he watched them go, helpless to stop them with a now screaming baby in his arms.

I grimaced. The guy was trying. That much was clear. But he was way out of his league.

Uninvited, I got out of the car and rescued the bottles from beneath a bush. Noting his pure relief as I strode past him, I went to the door and opened it, not needing a key, because nobody out here ever locked their doors. I stepped aside so he could enter, and tried not to notice the rush of memories I got from being back again.

We’d had good times here, back when his parents had owned this house. Riding horses. Lying in the hammock in the yard, talking about what our lives would be after high school. I’d missed those quiet moments most of all.

“Thank you,” he said for about the five hundredth time in the past twenty-four hours.

“You gotta stop saying that.”

“I know, but I mean it. I don’t know what I would have done without you last night. Or today.” He paused, and his gaze met mine. “I don’t know what I’ve done without you the last four years.”

My breath whooshed out of me like a freight train. What the hell? “Nate, I—”

Then Molly’s screams started up again, killing the moment. I jerked my head away without responding to his admission.

Nate took Molly in the direction of the bedrooms, presumably in search of fresh clothes, and I headed for the kitchen, dumping the dirty bottles to the side of the sink and twisting on the hot water to wash them out. I didn't think Molly would wait for me to run the dishwasher. I made the water as hot as I could stand and plunged my hands in, scrubbing out the bottle thoroughly.

What had he meant when he'd said he didn't know what he'd done without me the last four years? Did that mean he'd missed me? Or just he'd missed having someone around to help him when he was in a jam? I was sure he had friends on the tour. Girlfriends, probably. I knew there had to be a ton of women throwing themselves at him. He was a young, good-looking cowboy, in the spotlight of a worldwide tour. He had the bad-boy, adrenaline-junkie appearance that most women fell for in a heartbeat. I'd seen the posters and I'd watched the interviews. He played his part well, full of swagger and confidence, with the occasional yes ma'am thrown in to prove he was a sweetheart with small-town manners. I could still see glimpses of the boy I'd known, but they'd been buried beneath his public persona. I didn't know him anymore. I didn't know what was real and what was made up for the fans.

So I concentrated on making Molly her bottle. I read the instructions on the formula packet, heating the water in the microwave before adding the powder then shaking it vigorously to combine them. When Nate appeared with the cleaned up, but still angry baby, I passed him the bottle.

He poked it into Molly's open mouth, but she just kept on wailing.

"Sit. She probably needs to lie down."

He did as I suggested, but after a minute of him attempting to get her to take the bottle with no luck, he looked up at me in dismay. "What am I doing wrong?"

I honestly had no idea. "Here, let me try."

I took the very distressed Molly and tucked her tight to

my body like I had in the hospital, her head resting in the crook of my elbow. "Hey, sweet girl. You gotta drink this, okay? It's good."

I did exactly what Nate had done and poked the bottle in Molly's mouth. She immediately clamped down on it and suckled.

Silence fell over the room, and it was blissful. I relaxed back into the worn couch, grateful she was drinking. Her little eyes were already fluttering. "She'll be out like a light before she finishes this," I predicted.

Nate inched closer, leaning across me to study her face.

I froze. His body pressed against my arm, and if he swiveled his head a fraction, his face would be within kissing distance.

"Yeah, you're right. Poor kid. All that screaming had to be tiring."

I could barely make sense of what he was saying. My brain had gone on full code blue alert with sirens and flashing lights, all of them alerting me to the fact Nate could kiss me right now, if only he wanted to.

He turned in my direction.

And for half a second, I lost my head. My gaze flickered to his lips, then back up before I realized what I'd done.

Nate didn't want me. Not like that. He'd made that clear.

I jerked back, though I couldn't go far with the couch at my back. Four years should have dulled all those unwanted feelings. But they hadn't. They'd just been lying dormant, waiting for him to return.

I couldn't stand being this close to him.

So I changed tactics and stood, practically taking Nate out with the end of Molly's bottle in the process. It caught him in the fleshy part below his eye, and he flinched, clapping his hand over the injury.

"Fu—"

"Ah!" I stopped him in a whisper-shout. "Don't swear!"

"Buck! What are you doing? That hurt."

What was I doing? I had no idea. I looked down at Molly, asleep in my arms, the bottle having fallen from her lips. "Sorry. I just wanted to put her to bed." Yeah, good excuse. I wanted to put her to bed so much I'd moved as if a rattlesnake had bitten me on the ass. Smooth, Hallie. Smooth.

Didn't that just define me now? Curse my stupid feelings. Before they'd made themselves known, I'd never had any of this awkwardness with Nate. But then one day in our senior year of high school, something had changed. It wasn't even something big, like accidentally seeing him naked or watching him date another girl. Mr. Goven had called on Nate during our shared math class, and Nate had thrown me a wink as he'd walked past my desk.

That was it. The one single, solitary moment I could pinpoint, where my feelings for Nate had gone from brotherly to 'do me now.'

Embarrassment curled its way up from the depths of my stomach, and I took off for the hallway to the bedrooms, searching for Molly's nursery. Anything to put a bit of space between me and Nate.

Taking an educated guess that it would be the old spare bedroom, I turned in and shut the door behind me, giving myself a minute. "Your uncle is going to think I've completely lost it," I whispered to the sleeping baby. I put the bottle down on the dresser and then dropped a soft kiss on to Molly's head. I couldn't help it. I felt somehow bonded to her, after everything we'd been through last night, and without her mom here to give her a kiss goodnight, someone had to.

I placed her down in her crib and took a deep breath, pulling back my shoulders. Okay, so I'd just maimed, then run away from the guy I'd been harboring feelings for. So what? I could still go out there with my head held high.

Then straight out the door, because obviously I couldn't be trusted in close spaces with him.

Nate had other ideas. His gaze slammed into mine the minute I appeared from the bedroom.

"What was that?"

"What?" I asked, though I knew exactly what he was talking about.

"It was like I electrocuted you."

That wasn't far from the truth. There had been a distinct sparking feeling as he'd touched me. I needed to change the subject. Or leave. But he was blocking the doorway, and I definitely didn't trust myself to get any closer to him.

"How long are your sister and Shep going to be in hospital for?"

He cocked his head to one side, as if I'd said something curious, but eventually he went with it and answered me. "Not sure. Weeks. Maybe longer."

"What about the ranch?"

His teeth sank into his bottom lip as he gazed out the window. It was getting dark outside, the sun partially dipping below the horizon and casting the Mathews' vast property in sunset colors. I wandered to the window and gazed out, amazed by the beauty.

I fought back a flinch as Nate came to stand beside me, and instead focused on the stunning display in front of me, rather than the stunning display next to me.

Goddamn him. Why did he have to be so attractive? Why did he have to come back at all? It was so much easier for me when he wasn't around. Sure, I had to deal with missing him, which still took up almost every second of every day, even after four years apart, but that was still somehow easier than having him back home.

"I guess I'll work it. At least until they can hire someone."

I shot him a glance. "You remember how?"

He rolled his eyes at me. "Yes, smart-ass. I might have been away, but that doesn't mean the cowboy in me is lost forever."

I couldn't help but tease him over that. "You sure? Riding a horse for hours a day is a little different to riding one of your bulls for a measly eight seconds."

He nudged me playfully, but this time, I was more prepared for it, and it didn't freak me out quite so much when that distinct ripple of attraction spread up my arm.

"I think I can handle it."

"What about Molly, though?"

He drifted back to the couch and flopped down into it, scrubbing a hand through his hair. "Honestly, I don't know. I guess I'll just take her with me."

I gaped at him. "While you're feeding cows and sheep and fixing fences? What are you going to do, just attach her stroller to the back of your horse?"

"I was thinking I'd put her in one of those strappy things that go on your back."

I blinked. "Are you serious right now? How on earth did anyone give you temporary custody of this child?"

He seemed genuinely confused. "What? No good?"

I spotted the 'strappy thing' in question and tossed it at him. "If you can get it on, you can do it."

His mouth lifted at the corner in an adorable grin, and he pushed to his feet. Had he always been so much taller than me? Or was it that he'd filled out so he just felt bigger?

"Ye of little faith. I got this."

He didn't. And I knew it. But I was here for the amusement factor of watching him try and fail.

He held up the contraption, and I saw the minute his confidence faltered. He turned it upside down, studying it. He lifted one strap and put it over his shoulder, but the thing was a mess of buckles and levers, not to mention the fact it was obviously way too small for his big body. Still, he amused me while he tugged at it.

It took his arm getting stuck behind his back for him to admit defeat. "Fine. This thing was a dumb idea. Want to help me out here?"

I almost didn't want to, just because it was so amusing. But I stood and grabbed the strap caught around his arm, moving it and undoing buckles and loops that crisscrossed over his body. I had to move to his front to get the last one, and as it dropped to the floor, I became aware of how close we were.

I stared at the logo on his T-shirt, willing myself to move away, but it was like a magnet pulled me in his direction, too strong for me to fight off. His fingers brushed my arm, then slid lower over my palm, until his fingers wound between mine.

"Thank you," he said softly, voice barely more than a whisper.

"I told you to stop saying that."

He inched closer. "I know. But I don't know what else to say. I don't know how to say all the things I really mean. Not when you can't even look at me."

My breath hitched. If I lifted my head, his lips would be right there. His so very kissable lips that I'd imagined myself tasting over and over.

I wouldn't be able to resist them.

So no, I couldn't look at him. I couldn't let him see I was still that seventeen-year-old girl on prom night, ready to give her virginity to a boy who only saw her as a friend. I couldn't be that vulnerable with him again. He'd broken my heart once already, and he'd do it again. This wasn't his life anymore, here in this little town with me. He'd outgrown it. He'd outgrown *me*. And I knew it.

When I walked away without meeting his gaze, he didn't stop me.

8

NATE

My phone woke me, it's shrill ring blasting through the early morning sunshine of my bedroom window. For a brief moment, I just blinked in the glare, wondering why I was groggy, before I remembered I'd been awake half the night trying to settle Molly. She'd only just dozed off again around four, and I'd crashed hard, completely exhausted.

I dove on my phone, praying it hadn't already woken the beast. A cute beast, to her credit, but a beast nonetheless.

"Hello?"

Sobbing came down the line, and my stomach sank like a lead ball in the ocean. Fear gripped my throat. "Jas? Talk to me. What's happened?"

"Shep." Her sobs drowned out anything else she was trying to say.

The room spun, and I clamped my arm over my eyes. "Oh, fuck. No."

"Don't swear! He's good. That's what I'm trying to tell you. I mean he's not. He's beat to hell and had two surgeries, but he's awake. He's talking and he recognized me when they let me in to see him." She sniffed, and her tears gave way to relieved laughter. "Oh God, Nate. I really thought I was going to lose him."

I collapsed back against my bed, relief loosening every tense muscle until I laughed with her. I'd never been so glad of anything in my life. My breaths slowly returned to normal, and I assured Jasmine I'd bring Molly up to the hospital to see her and Shep once she woke up.

After I said goodbye, I lay quietly and listened to the silence, making sure Molly wasn't awake. When there was no gurgling or crying from the nursery, I closed my eyes again. But the adrenaline rush of Jasmine's call had left me wide awake, though I already knew I'd be flagging by early afternoon. But that was a problem for future Nate.

My gaze flickered around my bedroom. It was exactly the same as I'd left it. I didn't think Jasmine and Shep ever came in here, and I'd been away so long it was still a shrine to my teenage years. The bed still had the Atlanta Falcons bedspread, and my walls were full of photos and buckles from my early bull riding competitions. I stopped at the photo of me and Hallie sitting on the fence at the bull riding school where I'd done all my training. I smiled. It had been the beginning of our senior year of high school. I'd been doubling down on training, so she'd often come to watch, just so we could see each other.

I realized now that the amount of time she'd spent out there with me wasn't 'normal' friendship type behavior. But I hadn't seen that at the time. I'd just liked being around her. And I liked riding bulls. I'd had the two things I loved the most, and I hadn't thought about it any deeper than that.

I should have seen her feelings had changed.

But I hadn't. Not until it was too late.

Molly stirred in her crib, but this time I was grateful. It

gave me a reason to walk away from the memories that were too hard to think about.

Molly was a complete angel all day Sunday. She was in her element with both her parents around her again and had seemed completely unconcerned by their bandages and winces of pain, every so often, when she tried to climb on them. We hung out at the hospital from the minute she woke up, until dusk started settling and the nurses tossed us out. One pulled me aside at the nurses' station and asked that we only come for half the day tomorrow, because they didn't want Shep and Jasmine overexerting themselves.

The bad mood that descended on the baby beast as soon as we left the hospital in Jasmine's truck was just the beginning of the night from hell. Jasmine had been given the all clear to breastfeed during the day, which Molly seemed to prefer over the bottles and mushy baby food I kept offering her at home. She smeared food all through her hair instead of eating it, so I got a crash course in how to bath and wash the hair of a baby who hated your guts.

That was fun. And the night was no better, with Molly waking every two hours, then taking forty minutes to resettle.

By Monday morning, I'd sworn off having kids of my own. Ever. I downed two coffees in a row while the she-devil mouthed at a teething breadstick thingo that I'd found in the pantry. I skirted my way around where she sat on the floor, being careful not to get too close to her in case I set her off again.

I'd planned on getting outside today and seeing what

needed doing around the ranch. I knew Shep had just got in a big roll of fencing wire, making me think there might be fences down or in need of replacing, but I already knew from the last two days that Molly wasn't going to let me do any of that. "Sorry, Shep," I muttered to myself. "But until I can find someone to watch your daughter, the fences are just going to have wait."

The teething stick hit me in the back of the leg, and Molly's accompanying cry of anger followed. I sighed, scooping her up from the floor, though that only seemed to make her worse. "Okay then. We need to get out of this house and kill some time before we go see your parents. Want to go see where Uncle Nate learned to ride bulls?"

She squawked some more, but that was her response to everything, so I bundled her stroller into the back of Jasmine's truck and made the short drive to the Hunt's property. I'd been meaning to come out here and see my old coach ever since I'd gotten back, and now the familiar dirt track that led to his farmhouse was like coming home.

I bypassed the house and drove around to the back, skirting the bull pens to park the truck with a row of other vehicles outside the training arena. Frost looked up from his perch on the top of a fence and held a hand up to shield his eyes from the sun. Summer and her mom waved us over, and the three of them got down as we approached.

Kai, my old coach, who everyone called Frost, gave me one of his rare smiles and stuck his hand out. "Long time no see, kid."

His eyes were even bluer than mine were, and despite his almost always sober expression, his eyes turned up at the corners. I was glad to see him, too. He'd been my first coach and the man who'd got me to the WBRA. I owed him my career, but he'd taught me so much more over the years.

My dad had passed when I was fourteen, and Frost had stepped in and taken on that mentor role for me.

I repaid him by working hard and abiding by the one rule he'd set.

No fooling around with his daughters.

It hadn't been a problem for me. I had my eye on the prize, and girls hadn't really been something I'd been paying much attention to. Frost's younger daughters were too young, and Summer was my age but more like a sister to me anyway. She was just one of the guys, working and training at the ranch like the rest of us. I certainly hadn't seen her in that light.

I hadn't seen anyone in that light. Not even when someone had been right under my nose.

"Nate Mathews! What on earth are you doing here after all these years?" Mrs. Hunt strained up onto her toes and kissed my cheek, smiling at me fondly, her dark eyes shining. She hadn't changed a bit since I'd been gone, her brown skin barely showing a wrinkle, despite the fact she had to be close to fifty. "And you brought our Molly girl. Hey there, sweetheart."

Molly gave her a gummy grin. Typical. She smiled for everyone but me.

"Good to see you, Mrs. Hunt."

She tapped me on the shoulder. "You're a grown-up man now. You can call me Addie."

I nodded, but we both knew I wouldn't. She'd always be Mrs. Hunt to me.

"Hey, again, Nate." Summer had a mischievous twinkle in her eye. "Get back from the hospital okay the other day?"

I tried to fight back a smile. "Yes, thanks. It worked out well." Sort of. At least it had until Hallie had run off.

Like she'd read my mind, Summer raised an eyebrow. "Did you know Hallie works here?"

"Excuse me?"

"We missed having her around the place after you went on tour. So we gave her a job."

My heartbeat picked up. I had definitely not known that. How would I? Hallie had no social media under her legal name. I'd checked regularly over the years, as realization of my true feelings for her had grown. I'd asked my sister about her once or twice when I'd called, but she hadn't known anything. I'd fought off the urge to ask her to find out.

I hadn't expected to see Hallie today. But now I knew it was a possibility, I was going to make it happen.

"Uh, Frost?" a timid voice interrupted.

A trio of Frost's bull riders stood off to one side, their hats in hands.

"Uh-oh," I said with a laugh. Because I knew that look. These kids had to be no more than sixteen or seventeen, and it hadn't been that long since I'd been the one in their position. They had that air of fear about them, the one teenagers got when they had royally fucked up and were now having to face the music.

Frost knew it, too. "What have you done?"

"There's a bull out."

Frost's growl kinda scared me, and it wasn't even aimed in my direction.

Summer narrowed her eyes at them. "Which one?"

"Grave Digger."

"Fuc—" Summer shot a glance at Molly and gritted her teeth. "*Bucking* cowboys."

Bucking cowboys, indeed.

9

HALLIE

There wasn't enough work to be done. I'd gotten to work early and had been flogging myself half to death all morning without stopping for a break. Who needed breakfast, when breakfast meant stopping for long enough that you had time to think about the stupid mess you'd made at Nate's place on Saturday night?

I couldn't stop thinking about the way his fingers had slid between mine. Such a simple gesture, and yet it had been ginormous to me. I was sure we'd held hands from time to time during high school. Surely I'd tried to drag him somewhere and had grabbed him by the hand to do it. But if I had, I couldn't remember it. And it couldn't have felt the way it did on Saturday night.

I groaned and leaned against one of the horse stalls that I'd just cleaned out and lined with fresh straw. "Why am I so bucking useless around him?" There was no one around to hear me, and I snorted on a laugh that I'd said bucking instead of cursing. It had a ring to it. And hey, it fit my surroundings.

The clip-clop of horse's hooves on the wooden floor

stopped me, and I stuck my head out of the stall, wondering which horse it was and who was bringing it back. Smoke break wasn't over for another ten minutes, and while the ranch hands were hard workers, they weren't *that* eager.

I counted the horses as I went, mentally ticking off the list. The ranch only kept a handful, since their primary business was bull riding and cattle. Six heads hung over their stalls, staring at me curiously. Weird. They were all here and accounted for. But maybe we were babysitting a new horse. The Hunts had a lot of land here, so sometimes we took in boarders, when other locals were having trouble feeding or housing their animals.

I brushed off my hands on my jeans and tried to straighten my shirt. There wasn't much I could do about the dirt, but I could at least try to appear presentable if there was a new owner here with their animal. I strode around the corner, ready with a smile to greet them.

"Whoa. You're not a horse."

The massive bull looked up from the small pile of feed he'd found on the ground. His big body blocked the main entrance to the barn almost entirely, with only a sliver of space either side.

Definitely not enough room for me to try to make an escape.

I frowned at the beast who was eyeing me curiously. "What are you doing out of your pen and all alone? Those dumbass cowboys leave your gate open again?"

Grave Digger snorted.

I cringed. That didn't sound like a friendly sort of greeting. "I really hope your name is only for show. It is, right? You aren't gonna put me six foot under?"

His foot stamp and the annoyed toss of his head didn't instill much courage in my theory. Okay, time to get the hell outta here. I reversed, walking slowly backward through the space between the horse stalls, aiming for the rear entrance. "Nice bull," I said quietly, adrenaline spiking as he pawed at the ground. "No need for charging. You just—"

I grunted in surprise when I backed right into something solid.

"Having a nice chat with your pal there?"

I closed my eyes for the briefest of moments when I recognized Nate's voice. Then realized that was a very dumb idea, when I was facing off with a bull who was thinking about mowing me down.

"We're just getting to know each other. Slightly too intimate a setting for a first date, though, if I'm honest. The guy is kinda all up in my personal bubble."

"Mind if I join in?"

"Actually, I think it's time to dine and ditch. My date is a bit of a dud." I strained to keep my concentration on the bull in front of me. But it was hard when I kept getting distracted by Nate's body pressed against my back. I could feel the rise and fall of chest, and his fingertips glanced over my hips, like he was ready to hoist me up and over his shoulder at any second.

Grave Digger put his head down, his huge horns scraping along the sides of the barn walls like nails down a chalkboard.

"Buck," Nate muttered. His fingers encircled my wrist. "Run."

We spun in unison, Nate dropping my wrist only long enough for me to turn before he picked it up again. We both hauled ass down the passageway, legs pumping. Grave Digger's snorts and hooves echoed off the rafters, instilling a fear in me I hadn't even known before. "This is not how I expected to die!"

I pushed my legs harder, gunning for the back entrance, but the bull was surprisingly quick for a great hulking animal, and it gained ground rapidly. A bucketful of feed fell from a post as we ran by, clattering to the ground beneath his hooves but did nothing to slow Grave Digger down.

My life flashed before my eyes, but it was all images of Nate and me. The two of us at a rodeo. Him swimming at the dam. That night at prom where I'd ruined it all.

I wished I could take it back.

It would have been better to have had him as friend all this time than to have lost him the way I had.

"Nate!" I yelled, no idea what I was actually going to say next. I love you? Did I? I had, once upon a time. I felt like I had to say something if this was how I was going out, gored to death by some asshole bovine who would have been better off as steak.

A sharp tug on my wrist had me falling to the right. Down I went, crashing into Nate, who fell hard into the ground. I squeezed my eyes tight and braced myself for the impact of Grave Digger's horns through my spleen. Did you need a spleen to live? I had no idea. Even if you didn't, this wasn't going to tickle.

A moment passed, and the pain didn't come. I opened one eye.

With a bellow of rage, Grave Digger stormed past the horse stall Nate had pulled me into, the one I'd just spent twenty minutes cleaning out and filling with fresh straw.

I sucked in a deep breath, grateful I still could and that my lungs hadn't been turned into Swiss cheese. My heart rate slowed, and it was only then I realized I was lying fully on top of the man I'd had a crush on for the past four years.

Aaaand back up my blood pressure went.

I rolled off him quickly but only got as far as the straw

beside him. I couldn't bring myself to get up. My heart pounded so hard the effort of standing would have surely made it explode.

"What were you going to say?" Nate asked, breathing hard.

My eyes widened, and I remembered I'd almost blurted out my feelings. Fear of being jabbed in the ass cheek with a horn had that sort of effect on me apparently. "Nothing! I was just going to point out this empty horse stall here would be a good diversion, but you knew what you were doing. No need for me to say anything." I laughed, but it wasn't lost on me that it sounded slightly hysterical. Whether that was because of the near organ skewering, or because I was lying so close to Nate Mathews, I had no idea. I was acutely aware that our arms were touching, and the pulse I felt from the places our skin met had me tingling.

I needed to make that stop before I opened my big mouth again. "I suppose we should get up and alert the others that there's a bull on the loose."

I tried to sit as Grave Digger's hooves disappeared into the distance, but Nate's fingers were still wrapped around my wrist. He pulled me back down, his breath a sharp inhale.

Surprise ricocheted through me. "Uh, Nate?"

He stared straight up at the rafters. "Hallie."

"What are we doing?"

"They already know about the bull."

"Okay, but why are we still on the ground?"

His head swiveled in my direction, and his gaze froze me in place. There was a heat behind it I'd never seen before, and it kindled something inside me that burned away my fear, leaving nothing but a smoldering need.

What the hell was going on here?

His gaze dipped to my lips, just like mine had with him on Saturday night, and my mouth fell open. I put a hand up and clapped it over his eyes. "Whoa. What the hell are you doing? Don't do that!"

He chuckled and pried my fingers away from his face. "Do what?"

"You looked at my mouth!"

"Yeah, so?"

Yeah, so? What the hell? "Do you not know that's the universal signal for 'kiss me'?"

He screwed his face up. "It is?"

"Yes! And you just did it to me!"

His gaze dropped to my lips again. "Like this?"

"Yes! Stop it!"

His mouth turned up at the corners, and that smirk that drove me a little bit mental curved his lips. "What if I don't want to?"

Irritation spiked in my blood, and I tried to sit up again. "Stop it, Nate. It's not funny. Don't make fun of me."

The amusement fell right off his face. "Hey, I'm not."

I shoved at his chest, trying to put some distance between us, but he was like a trampoline and bounced right back into my personal space.

This was mortifying. "I know I made a fool of myself on Saturday night. Just like I did at prom. Apparently, it's just something I do around you, no matter how old we get."

I pushed to my feet, but Nate was quicker. He shot up, his big body blocking the only exit to the stall, much the same way Grave Digger had. Only this time, when Nate advanced on me, I didn't move back.

"Hallie. Look at me."

I couldn't do that. I refused to let him see how much his

actions had hurt me. Embarrassment had my blood hot, and all I wanted to do was sink into the floor.

His finger traced down the side of my face and trailed beneath my chin, forcing it up.

It only pissed me off more. Couldn't he just go let me lick my wounds in private?

So I let him see it. The fire in my eyes that told him exactly how angry I was. At myself more than him, really. I just kept doing this same old thing every time I was around him. I couldn't seem to stop, and it was excruciating.

"I know what staring at your lips means." His gaze flickered to my mouth again. "I know *exactly* what it means. How many times do I have to do it before you say I can kiss you?"

The breath whooshed out of me on a sharp exhale. I searched his gaze for a sign he was lying or making fun of me. But this time, there wasn't a hint of amusement in his expression.

He was dead serious.

That was suddenly terrifying.

"I can't," I said, pushing off him.

The hurt in his eyes nearly floored me, but I had to get out of there and put some space between us. I didn't know Nate anymore. Everything he did just confused me more. I'd been thinking about him kissing me for four years, knowing it would never happen. He couldn't just waltz back into town and start saying he was actually going to do it.

That wasn't how this worked. "I don't want to."

"No," he called, scrambling after me. "Bullshit, Hallie. I don't buy that."

I froze in the doorway, but I didn't turn around. When his big body closed in on me, a tremble rocked me from tip to toe.

He bent his head so his lips hovered just over my ear. "I

fucked up. I was a stupid kid who had blinders on. All I saw was bull riding, and partying, and getting out of this town. You were my best friend, and I didn't realize something had changed for you. I had no idea what you were going to do that night."

I let out a shaky breath, relieved I wasn't facing him. The mortification from that evening came rushing back, and I was that same seventeen-year-old kid all over again, throwing herself at a boy who didn't want her. "I blindsided you. I know that. I should have talked to you."

"Maybe. But I should have seen it. I knew you better than anyone." His fingers gripped my arms, and he spun me around. "Dammit, Hallie. I would have never organized that party if I'd known. You have to know that. I never wanted to hurt you."

Shame heated my cheeks when I remembered the stares and laughter. It was still as clear as day in my head. Me lying in what I thought was a seductive pose across the hotel bed, my boobs spilling out of cheap lingerie, expecting Nate to walk in, take one look at me, and rip his clothes off, too.

Instead, I got a whole group of teenage boys, ready for an afterparty. And a flat-out rejection from my best friend.

"I was stupid."

"You were beautiful."

Oh goddammit. Why did he have to say things like that? I lifted my gaze to meet his.

"You still are. If I could have a do-over, I would. If I could do it all again, I would have read the signs. I would have never invited my friends up to the room. It would have just been you and me." He moved in closer so our chests touched. His head dipped again, so his mouth hovered over mine, his warm breath tickling my lips.

"I would have told you the moment I saw you on that

bed, you switched from being my best friend to something entirely different."

He inched forward again, guiding me until my back hit the barn wall. I was completely powerless to stop him, not that I wanted to. This was all my teenage fantasies come true. My legs had turned into jelly, and there was a real danger of me melting into a puddle if he stopped using his body to press me into the wall.

Nate leaned in so far that I anticipated his kiss, my eyes fluttering closed. But it didn't come. Instead he changed course, running his nose along my jawline before trailing his lips to the sensitive spot beneath my ear.

Oh God. I was going to incinerate.

"I would have kissed you here." His lips traced down my neck, just barely touching me. "And here."

Nate ground against me, his dick thickening behind his jeans. "And then I would have told you that in just one glimpse, I'd never been so hard."

I moaned quietly, unable to stop it.

"So when I ask you again if I can kiss you, just remember you aren't the only one who wants this. Got it?"

I've never answered so quick in my life. "Yes," I breathed. "Yes. Yes. Okay."

He pulled back abruptly, forcing me to catch myself on my wobbly legs. My eyes flew open.

He smirked. "I didn't ask again."

My mouth dropped open as he walked away.

He threw me a cocky grin over his shoulder. "But don't worry, I will."

10

HALLIE

It took me a good ten minutes to get my breathing, not to mention my libido, to calm down. I hid in the barn, fanning myself with a newspaper I found on Frost's desk, like I was out of some 1960's movies where the women swooned and fell at men's feet.

I definitely had some swooning going on. I'd slept with guys in the years he'd been gone, but none of them had ever made me feel what I'd just felt with Nate. And he'd barely touched me.

When I finally thought my cheeks were no more pink that normal, I slipped from the barn and headed for the training ring, where a crowd had gathered to watch the trainees practice. Nate's tall frame and broad shoulders were the first things I noticed, Molly high in his arms. But he was talking to Frost about one of the trainees, so I grabbed a spot on the rail next to Summer. Inside the ring, a young cowboy, in a hat that looked too big for him, tried desperately to hold on to a bull that was barely kicking. I winced.

Summer elbowed me. "Quit being so obvious. This lot is

brand-new and they're terrible, but their money is as good as anyone's."

She had that right. These wannabes paid my wages, so I politely clapped when the guy fell off, landing in the dirt with a thud.

Frost motioned the kid over to him and Nate, and the two of them explained in-depth what had gone wrong.

I couldn't help but watch Nate. Frost was quiet and to the point, but Nate was outgoing and chatted with the kid, reassuring him he was that bad once, too.

I didn't think he was, but at least the kid walked away smiling.

Molly whined and fidgeted, seemingly bored with standing still, and Nate paced over to me, trying to distract her. "So, Molly wants to know if you want to come over for dinner with her tonight?"

I jumped down from the fence and wiped my hands off on the back of my jeans. "Does she now?"

Molly squawked and tried to throw herself backward out of Nate's arms. He put her down to crawl around our feet and turned a sheepish grin on me. "Okay, fine. Molly didn't ask. She's super rude like that. But I'm asking."

I raised an eyebrow, remembering his earlier promise. As if I could forget. "Asking what exactly?"

His gaze darkened, and his smile turned cocky. "Right now, I'm asking you to come over to my place for a meal. Maybe after I'll have more questions."

I couldn't help but grin. "Fine. Dinner and questions sound good."

Frost cleared his throat. "If you two are done flirtin', your baby is eating cowshit."

"What!" Nate spun in a circle, looking for Molly who'd crawled away.

"Oh my God," I burst out laughing when I spotted her. She had cowshit smeared over her hands and face.

"Molly!" Nate rushed over, picking her up, holding her out away from his body. He widened his eyes at me in a panic, clearing out her mouth. "Is this bad? Do I need to take her to the doctor?"

I shrugged. I had no idea.

Molly gave him the gummiest grin and clapped her hands happily at him.

"Hey, at least she likes you right now."

He frowned, but Molly's happiness was infectious. Slowly a grin spread across his face, wiping out his worried expression. "Is that all I had to do to get you to like me? Let you eat some poop?" He turned to the rest of us watching them. "Seriously, though? Do I call an ambulance?"

Addie, Summer's mom, swept in and plucked Molly from Nate's outstretched arms. "You think I raised three girls on this farm without each of them tasting a little cow poo once or twice? They lived to tell the tale. You're just fine, aren't you, baby girl? Let's get you cleaned up." She headed for the house but then called over her shoulder, "Nate, I'll take Molly tonight for you. Who knows what she'll eat next if you and Hallie are...distracted again."

My cheeks went pink once more, but this time, I didn't mind so much.

That night after work, I stayed in the shower until the water ran cold. Which wasn't really all that long, because the hot water heater in my ancient home was tiny, outdated, and in dire need of replacement.

Just like practically everything else in the house.

But that wasn't going to get me down tonight. I'd shaved everything, exfoliated, moisturized, and even thrown a little fake tan on so my T-shirt lines from working outdoors all day weren't quite as noticeable when I was naked.

I swallowed thickly. If I was being honest, I was preparing for Nate to see me in my birthday suit, and the excitement of where the night might lead went straight to my head. By the time I got to Nate's front door, I felt slightly drunk.

I knocked and waited with my heart pounding. It seemed ridiculous that I was suddenly so nervous, considering I'd stood in this exact position a million times over the years. But only once before had I stood here wearing a pretty outfit, thinking the night would end with Nate and I becoming a whole lot more than friends.

It hadn't played out like that last time, but things were different now. We were older. More experienced. I didn't have to make this into some epic fantasy. He was leaving again. I knew that. So a relationship wasn't on the table. But sex was. And after the way Nate had pressed up against me in the barn, letting me feel the effect I had on him, there was no doubt in my mind anymore that we were on the same page.

Holy crap.

"You just gonna stand out there all day?" Nate called through a window.

Well, that was a great start. Without knocking, because what was the point, the man obviously knew I was here, I twisted the door handle and let myself in. I found him in the kitchen, a delicious aroma wafting out from the oven. He straightened from checking on whatever it was he had cooking and turned to me. His gaze rolled over my body so slowly it was almost indecent. When he finally made it back up to my eyes, there was a fire behind them that made me glad I'd spent so long getting ready.

It also made me kind of desperate to get out of these clothes and underneath him.

But we were still kind of feeling our way around this whole switch from friends, to not talking, to something new, and I wasn't brave enough to suggest we skip dinner entirely. Even if my libido was being a bossy bitch and constantly reminding me I needed to fulfil all my high school fantasies in the very short amount of time he had left here. Instead, I yanked open the refrigerator door. "Wine? Please tell me you have wine." I stared into the shelves and drawers of food without really seeing any of them.

He reached around me and plucked a bottle from the middle shelf, right in front of my eyes.

"Yeah, we have wine."

I let the cool refrigerator air wash over me for a moment, but eventually I had to face him.

He held out a glass, and I took it, jolting at brush of his fingers over mine.

He rested one hip on the edge of the countertop and grinned at me. "I have questions."

I choked on my wine. "Already?"

"Mmm hmm. It's been a long time since we last talked, and I need to be caught up on your life."

I shrugged, trying to hide my disappointment that he wasn't going to lead with the kissing question. "Nothing much to tell. Small-town girl and all that."

He rolled his eyes. "You think that isn't interesting to me? Everything about you interests me, Hallie."

A thrill rolled down my spine. I didn't want to talk about myself, but he was staring at me like I'd climbed the world's highest mountains or performed intricate surgeries on celebrities. “Well, you already know I work over at the Hunts’ place.”

“Yeah, but I don’t know what you do.”

“I do whatever needs doing. Fix fences, clean stalls, feed animals. Sometimes I’m more of the receptionist, fending off worried parents who have sent their kids here to learn how to ride but then freak out every time said kid falls off.”

“Ah yeah, I remember those kinds. The city slickers who came out for summer camps were the worst. But Frost always got ’em riding by the end.”

I took another sip of my wine. “He’s still the same. He has endless patience with them. Summer not so much, but she’s not teaching as often these days with how hard she’s training for the pros.”

“She’s going to qualify this year for sure. I’ve been following her career. She’s been so close the last two times.” The timer went off on the oven, and Nate paused to pull out a thick stew with hearty chunks of meat and vegetables.

My mouth watered. “That looks amazing.”

He put it down on the stove top. “Hopefully it tastes good, too. I haven’t cooked a proper meal in ages. It’s hard when we’re in hotels all the time, and when I come home at Christmas, I’m only here for forty-eight hours before I’m gone again. Doesn’t leave much time for anything but unwrapping gifts and eating whatever Christmas meal Jasmine has whipped up.”

This was news to me. I had no idea he’d been home at all. But of course he had.

He just hadn’t had the time or the inclination to come visit me.

That stung a little, but I wasn’t going to let him see. He’d had no responsibility to check in with me. We’d left on bad terms, and I’d ignored his calls for months after, too embarrassed to face him. Was it any surprise he hadn't tried to contact me after that? I didn't want to ruin tonight by rehashing all of that again.

He passed me a bowl from a top cupboard, and I tried not to drool when he uncovered the stew and ladled a healthy portion for me. He did the same with his own bowl, then grabbed a loaf of crusty bread, and we took the lot to the dining room table.

He cut the bread up, slathering butter on before dunking it in his stew. I followed suit, and we watched each other eat from across the table. The stew was delicious, and I had several bites before I could stop long enough to speak again.

"So tell me about your job then. It's much more exciting than mine. I want to hear all about it."

I'd expected him to talk animatedly about his time on the road, and the roar of crowds yelling his name at arenas all over the country. But he just lifted one shoulder. "Not much to tell."

I gaped at him. "You tour the world as a professional cowboy, risking your life every time you get on the back of a bull, but there's not much to tell?"

He shrugged. "It's just...mundane now, I guess, after all these years. I spend most of my time either on planes or in hotels. The rest of the time is spent getting my ass handed to me. I'm twenty-two and I feel like I'm one hundred some days. I can't even tell you how many injuries I've had."

I threw a bit of bread at him from across the table. "Get outta here. Stop playing your amazing life down because mine is so small. You get to see the world. Your fans scream your name. And you make bank."

"Only if I win."

"Which you do, regularly."

He raised an eyebrow. "You follow my career?"

Was stalking him religiously on every social media platform, under my generically named accounts so he wouldn't notice, and watching all his rodeos on TV following his career? It would be highly embarrassing to let him know I'd seen every ride he'd had since he'd left me. "I've seen bits and pieces here and there. You're kinda big news around here, you know. You win something, people talk. It's hard not to hear it."

He looked down and stabbed at his meat with his fork. "Right. I remember how the gossip hotline is around here. My turn to ask a question then, yeah?"

Now that I knew he wasn't going to be asking about kissing I was much more comfortable with the idea of his questions. "Sure."

"Where are you living now? You still at your folks' place?"

"Oh God no. I got outta there right after high school. I stayed at the Hunts' place for a while, in one of their cabins."

"Handy for work."

"Yeah, and it was practically like being roommates with Summer. We got close. She filled the void..." I clammed up. Because what I was going to say was that she'd filled the void in my life that he'd left.

He swallowed hard. "I glad you replaced me, Hallie. I'm glad Summer was there for you when I wasn't."

"I didn't *replace* you. I just...I don't know. You weren't here anymore, and I needed a friend."

He blew out a long breath. "I'm sorry for the way I left. I shouldn't have. I should have stayed and talked to you."

"No, you had to go. Your career is important. You couldn't just delay leaving because I was an idiot."

He sighed and stood, taking his empty bowl with him. He indicated to mine, and I passed it over. He carried them to the kitchen sink, then leaned on it, staring at me. "Can you stop beating yourself up over it? You weren't the one who was an idiot. And I hate hearing you talk badly about yourself."

I shrugged. If the shoe fit...

He grabbed the bottle of wine, and I stood, following him to the living room. He tossed a handful of Molly's toys into a basket, and we both settled onto the worn couch.

I ran a hand over the familiar material. It hadn't changed since the last time we'd sat here together. But we had, he and I. "My turn for a question?"

He shifted, as if uncomfortable. "I think I should get a bonus question for cooking dinner."

I raised an eyebrow. "You think?"

His expression relaxed into something more cocky. "Yep. My game, my rules."

I took another sip of my wine. "Fine. One more question, but then I get two."

He sobered. "Am I stepping on any toes by inviting you here tonight? I realized I kind of ambushed you earlier today, and I didn't even ask if there was a guy..."

I shook my head quickly. "No. No guy. What about you? You must have girls throwing themselves at you."

"Some," he admitted. "But none I've ever wanted to catch." He eyed me like there was more to his statement than just the words he'd spoken aloud.

My breath hitched. "What exactly does that mean?"

He inched closer and extracted the wine glass from my hand. "It means that every time I've even thought about dating someone, I compare them to you. And then I start thinking about how different my life could be right now, if instead of running off to join the rodeo, I'd just stayed."

The air punched from the room. "You mean, if you'd stayed...for me?"

His gaze flickered all over my face, from the tendrils of hair falling from my temples, across the freckles on my nose, and finally, to my lips. "You already had your two questions. It's my turn."

My pulse thrummed. "Oh, now you're a stickler for the rules?" I fought to keep my tone light and joking, when really, I was dying on the inside. The anticipation was killing me slowly, one question at a time. I cleared my throat, but my words still came out breathy. "Then ask."

Our gazes collided. His hand snaked to the back of my neck, and he pulled me closer so his lips hovered just over mine. "I don't think I want to ask anymore. I think I'm just going to do it."

Then he put his mouth on mine.

Suddenly it was like the last four years disappeared. There was no hurt, no confusion, no missing him.

It was just me and him, and a soul-deep connection that had me fisting my fingers into his shirt. Our lips parted, our tongues sliding together as he speared his fingers into my hair, holding me tight to him.

Holy hell, Nate could kiss. He moved with the same confidence he had on the back of the bull, taking control and owning it, branding me with his touch, and taking me higher with every stroke of his fingertips.

"Is it my turn for a question?" I asked between hot presses of his mouth.

But he kissed me again and then shook his head. "No, still mine."

More kisses that made my head spin and my thighs

clench together. I moved away, needing to breathe before I imploded. "Are you serious? How many questions do you get?"

His grin became cocky. "You just asked two more. So now it's definitely my turn."

I snorted on a laugh. "You don't play fair."

He pretended to think on that for a moment, then nodded. "You're right, I don't." He swept my hair to one side and leaned in, kissing the side of my neck. He trailed his tongue up toward my ear, circling it, then whispered. "I don't want to play fair with you, Hallie. Fair would mean you reciprocate whatever I do to you, right?"

I switched our positions and kissed his neck, my lips brushing over the dark blond stubble along his jaw. "Sure. I'm all for reciprocation." I darted my tongue out, tasting his skin and was rewarded with his fingers drawing me closer.

But then he pulled back. "But what if I'm too impatient? What if I just want to press you back into this couch and show you exactly how much I don't just want to be your friend? You gonna stop me?"

I grinned against his lips. "Fair is overrated anyway."

That was all the permission he needed. His palms skated down my arms, and over my thighs while he grinned wickedly at me.

"Nate..."

He yanked my legs, hauling my ass out from beneath me so I landed flat on my back on the couch. I barely even had time to laugh before he was rearing over me. "This is very unfriend-like," I whispered. As if on autopilot, my legs parted so he could kneel between them, and I hooked one over his waist, drawing him down so he was laid on top of me.

"Every time we sat here during senior year, is that what you were thinking about doing?"

I grinned at him. "Maybe. You regretting all those nights of video games now? How many nights did we sit here playing PlayStation?"

He buried his face in the spot where my neck met my shoulder and inhaled deeply. "You see now why it was me who was the idiot? So dumb." He sucked the sensitive skin of my neck, and tingles roared through my body.

I slanted my head, giving him better access. "So be smart now, then."

He pushed aside the neck of my top, placing hot, open-mouthed kisses across my collarbone, licking and nipping my skin as he went. He supported his weight on one forearm, but the other traced down the side of my breast, over the indent of my waist, and stopped at the flare of my hip. His fingers slipped beneath the fabric of my shirt, lifting it, until he brushed over the lacy cup of my bra. His lips found mine once more, and he kissed me soft and slow, drugging kisses that spun the room. When his hand cupped my breast, thumb flicking over my nipple, it was the most natural thing in the world to push him up so I could get my shirt off. I fisted his, too, urging him to get it over his head, suddenly desperate to see what I'd been missing all these years.

"Wow," I whispered as our shirts hit the floor.

My gaze tracked over his bronze skin, the muscles rippling beneath in his effort not to completely crush me with his weight. His body was sculpted perfection. I ran my fingers from his pecs to the ridges of his abs, to the V lines that ran either side of his low-belted jeans. He groaned as I got to his waistband. I paused there, running my fingers along the smooth planes of his abs, taunting myself with what lay below, just as much as I was taunting him. His erection bulged from behind his fly, promising a very good time if I let it free.

Nate didn't give me the chance. He grabbed my hands, pulling them up above my head and pinning them to the armrest. "Hold it. I said this wasn't going to be fair, and I didn't mean that I was going to be the one getting all the action."

I pouted.

But he kissed me again. "Don't let go."

The heat in his eyes had me nodding, and I was rewarded with him sitting back on his knees so he could palm both my breasts. He pinched my nipples between his thumb and forefingers, and I arched off the couch like I'd been electrified. I pretty much had. It had been so long since anyone had caressed me like this, and it just wasn't the same when I did it alone in my house. I had no one to hear me scream there, but there was also no one capable of making me scream in the first place.

Nate was different. I already knew it and I was still mostly clothed.

His gaze locked with mine, and then he slid my bra straps down my shoulders, drawing the cups of my bra lower too, freeing my breasts.

He sucked in a breath as I was bared to him, and pinched my nipples again.

I moaned, pushing up into his touch, wanting him to do it again.

"How long has it been since someone touched you like this, Hallie?" His fingers trailed absently across the swell of my breast.

"Too long."

"You like this?" Another squeeze of my nipple.

"Is that another question?"

He chuckled. "Good point. It was a stupid question anyway, because I know what the answer is."

He put his mouth to my breast and sucked the tip into his mouth, rolling it between his teeth. Forgetting my promise to hold on, I grabbed the back of his head, clutching him to me while I arched into him.

"Fuck," he muttered against my skin. "I can't wait to get between your legs if that's how you respond when I suck your nipples."

I groaned at the thought, and when he went straight for the button on my jeans, undoing them and slipping his fingers beneath, I moaned my encouragement.

His mouth alternated between my boobs, nipping and sucking, while his fingertip found my clit.

"Oh!" I cried out at the very first contact.

He rubbed it for a moment before dipping lower, plunging between my folds to gather my arousal. "You're so wet, Hallie."

"Yeah, well, you made me wait four years," I complained with a grin.

"I'll make it worth it."

I shivered at his promise, but then his tongue was delving inside my mouth again, driving me wild. I rotated my hips, encouraging him to work me harder, faster. His fingers slipped over my clit, making tiny circles that sent need coursing straight to my core.

"I need more," I moaned. I went for his jeans again, but he wouldn't let me, moving out of my way. Then he slid two fingers up inside me, and my eyes rolled back. "Oh my God."

I shoved my jeans and panties down over my ass, just low enough to give him better access.

"You're so hot like this, Hallie. Fuck me. I want to watch you come."

He was going to get his wish. I couldn't hold my orgasm back now if I tried. It built strong and fast, taking me higher than I could ever achieve alone. His fingers pumped inside me, hitting my G-spot perfectly with every thrust. His thumb worked my clit, and his gaze raked my body, taking in my every curve, the heat in his eyes plain for me to see.

He pinched my nipple again, harder this time, and my back arched straight off the couch.

"Nate!" I spiraled into oblivion. Pulses of light and sensation roared through my body as I clamped down on his fingers. "Oh!"

A throat clearing from somewhere near the front door froze us both in place.

"Oh is right. Oh my."

11

NATE

Hallie yelped from beneath me and scrambled to get her jeans and underwear back up her legs.

I stuck my head up like a meerkat, peering over the back of the couch.

In the doorway, and elderly couple gaped at me, their mouths hanging open. "Nathaniel?"

I raised a hand in awkward greeting and scuttled off Hallie in order to stand up. "Mr. and Mrs. Shepherd! I didn't realize you were here already! All the way from Australia and everything."

I scooped to pick up Hallie's shirt from the floor and tossed it at her. She'd gotten her pants done up and was now trying to get her tits back in her bra. Goddammit. I was so not ready for her to be all covered up again. I'd barely even started.

But Shep's parents crashing the party put a very distinct end to the sexy times. My erection had shriveled the moment I'd heard Mrs. Shepherd's voice, so at least I wasn't now greeting her with a significant bulge behind my fly. I hurried to where they'd frozen in the hallway, crossing my arms over my chest self-consciously. Where the hell was my shirt? But I couldn't worry about that now, I needed to distract them long enough that Hallie could get dressed. "So how was the flight? Long, I guess? Did you go to the hospital yet? Shep and Jasmine are doing so much better," I babbled, trying to keep their focus on me.

Mrs. Shepherd grimaced at me and lowered her voice. "We're so sorry, Nathaniel. We didn't realize you had...company."

Mr. Shepherd, who was too much like his son for his own good, winked at me. "Sounds like you were having a good time." He turned to his wife. "Shame you never keep me company like that anymore."

I laughed loudly to cover my mortification and prayed that Hallie hadn't heard any of it.

"Nate, let them in. You've got them tied up in the doorway like a steer needing branding." Hallie came up behind me, fully dressed and put together, though the blazing red in her cheeks and her dilated pupils gave away how embarrassed she was. Even still, she stood tall, holding her own, and stuck her hand out to Mrs. Shepherd. "I'm Hallie. Lovely to meet you."

Mrs. Shepherd took her hand with a smile, but then it fell. Her gaze darted to me, her eyebrows pulling together in a frown. "Not *the* Hallie?"

I wanted to groan. I really liked Shep's parents. I'd met them a few times over the years, and they'd even come to one of my rodeos, but right now, they were killing me. I'd just got Hallie past all that crap, and now they were bringing it up again.

Hallie's confidence faltered, and she darted a look at me. "*The* Hallie?"

Mrs. Shepherd patted her hand. "Our son told us all about your little mishap after prom, but it appears you and Nate have made up now, so I guess that's all water under the bridge. You're a bigger woman than me, though, sweetheart. I don't think I could have gotten past that one."

I clapped my hands together, trying to divert their attention. If I hadn't had manners drilled into me from an early age, I would have muzzled Mrs. Shepherd with a death stare. Instead, I forced a smile. "So, you're staying here?"

"Of course. Where's Molly?"

"With a friend."

"Right, well, we'll just take Shep and Jasmine's room since you're in the guest room."

I frowned at that. "It's my bedroom, not the guest room."

The older woman waved a hand around at that. "Oh, Nathaniel. You never come back here. We've slept in that room more in the past four years than you have."

She laughed, completely unaware of how those words ate at me. I knew I'd been away a lot, but bull riding was my job. I already felt guilty about how little I'd seen my sister, and now I felt even worse. But the woman just kept on going, digging my grave deeper.

"I guess you'll be back off on tour now? When do you leave?"

Hallie stiffened beside me.

I didn't want to answer, but everyone was staring at me. "Friday," I admitted.

Hallie turned away, but I didn't miss the bob in her throat as she swallowed hard. "I didn't realize you'd already planned your return trip."

I caught her hand. "I didn't. Not exactly. It's just when

the tour starts again. I was going to extend it to take care of Molly—"

"No need for that now," Mrs. Shepherd interrupted. "You've got your life to live, you can't be hanging around here looking after a baby and her injured parents. We've got that handled."

Mr. Shepherd patted me on the shoulder. "You need to get back out on tour. If you miss even a week, you're going to lose your ranking. I've been following your rides, and you're doing so well. We're real proud of you."

I had no idea what to say. Shep's parents meant well, but they had no idea how badly they were throwing me under the bus right now. I could only imagine what Hallie was thinking. And it likely wasn't anything good.

She sucked in a deep breath and smiled. "I'm going to get out of your hair. You should have some family time."

"Hallie, no. Stay." I reached out to grab her hand, but she shook me off.

"No, it's fine. It's getting late anyway, and the Shepherds are probably hungry."

"Starving!" Shep's dad boomed. "I've had nothing but plane food, then hospital food for the last two days. I'd kill for a proper meal."

She smiled at him. "You're in for a treat. Nate is a great cook."

Shep's parents filed into the kitchen, while Hallie let herself out into the night.

I ran to catch up with her. "Hey, are you okay?"

She smiled tightly, but it didn't reach her eyes. "Yeah, sure. Fine."

I didn't think she was, but I couldn't force her to tell me the truth either. "Okay," I said slowly. "If you're sure. I'm really sorry about this. I wasn't done."

She lifted one shoulder then got inside her car. She put one hand on the door and looked up at me. “I guess you are now, though.”

She closed the door and started the engine before I could even protest.

12

HALLIE

In a funk of my own creating, I got to work early the next day, needing the distraction from my own thoughts. I knew there'd be coffee in the main house. Addie always had a pot brewing for us, but I knew they'd all be asking how my night with Nate had gone and I just couldn't think about that anymore. I found Frost out in the barn and was grateful he wasn't the sort of guy who liked to chitchat.

He took one look at my face, though, and concern furrowed his brow. "Do I need to kill him?"

I'd forgotten how perceptive Summer's dad was. I guessed you got used to reading women when you had three daughters. "Not just yet. But I reserve the right to take you up on it at a date to be determined." I gave him a half smile. "What needs doing?"

"All the usual morning routine, but then I'm going to need you in the training ring. You good to be my rope man?"

"Of course." I smiled at the fact he hadn't changed the job description just because I was a woman. I'd known nothing much about bull riding when I'd started hanging out around here to watch Nate, but now I knew all the terms. You needed somebody at the top of the bucking chute to help tighten the ropes around the bull's middle. That was the rope man. And you needed someone else to pull the gates. Frost had taught me years ago how to perform both roles, and though I had no desire to get on the back of a bull myself, I was good for the support crew.

I busied myself with feeding and watering animals, mucking out stalls, cleaning hooves, and sweeping out the trailer. It was good, honest work, and the morning sun beat down on my back, soothing the stiffness in my muscles I hadn't been able to shake since last night.

They'd locked up the moment I'd truly realized I was nothing more to Nate than a potential one-night stand. Of course, I'd tried to warn myself that he was only in it for a couple of days, but as soon as someone had said it out loud, something inside me had died.

It was only then I realized I'd been hiding a tiny flame of hope.

So stupid. I shoved aggressively at a pile of dirt I'd made at the back of the trailer, pushing it over the edge with a savage stab of my broom. Of course he was going back on tour. So what else could I be to him, other than a good time? Last night had been fun. I loved being in his company again. Then he'd kissed me, and everything had just ratcheted up a notch. It felt so natural and easy with him. He'd played my body like he knew it intimately. Like he knew *me*. And for a bit there, I'd lost my head to the fairy-tale dreams I'd been harboring for years.

I should thank the Shepherds for interrupting and bringing me back down to earth.

At mid-morning, I abandoned my chores and headed for the training ring. I found Summer hanging around the bucking chutes, watching her dad with a group of people I didn't recognize. "Who're they?" I nudged her with my elbow.

She jumped, spinning in my direction. Her eyes were wide. "Shit, Hallie. Don't sneak up on a girl like that."

"Was hardly sneaking. You were just lost in thought. Who are they?" I asked again.

I'd never seen Frost quite so animated. His smile was ear to ear as he embraced a man about the same age he was, maybe late forties or early fifties. A tiny woman with long dark hair hugged him next, and Addie watched on, big grin on her face. A younger guy stood slightly behind the others, wide-brimmed hat on his head.

"*They* are the Wests. Old friends of my dad's from when he used to ride. See the older guy? That's Johnny. They toured together when he was with the WBRA. That's his wife, Isabel, and their kid, Dominic."

I raised my sunglasses to the top of my head. "Their kid? That ain't no kid."

Dominic had to be six foot four. His broad shoulders stretched the seams of his button-down shirt that was entirely too warm for this time of year. When he looked in our direction, I took in the stubble across his jawline, and his dark eyes. He raised a hand in greeting, and Summer waved.

"Yeah, I guess not. He's the same age as we are, from memory. I haven't seen them for years. They live in Wyoming."

"What are they doing here?"

"No idea. But I think we're about to find out."

Frost strode across the training ring in our direction, Dominic and Johnny following after him. "You both remember my daughter, Summer, right? And this is our lead hand, Hallie."

We both jumped down to greet the newcomers. I put my hand out to shake Johnny's, then Dominic's, and we exchanged pleasantries.

But Dominic's attention kept swaying to Summer. "Did you get shorter?"

"Pretty sure you just became a giant," she quipped. "You here to ride?"

"Yes, ma'am. You know it."

Summer beamed at me. "Let's get the man a bull then, huh?"

"Wait. Now?" Dominic asked.

Summer lifted one shoulder. "Sure, why not. No time like the present. I want to know if you're still as bad as you were last time you were here." She turned to me. "Last time he came out he thought he was better than me. Had to put him in his place."

Frost chuckled at that. "Ah, my daughter. Not competitive at all, are you?"

Dominic grinned at her, too. "That was not exactly my recollection of the last time I rode here, but sure. Let's do it. Get a bull in that chute, and I'll show you how much I've 'improved.'" He made air quotes as he said it, but there was a wide, friendly tilt to his lips that showed it was all in good fun. He smiled at Summer again, and I darted a look in her direction. Her grin was wide as she held his stare.

Whoa. I linked my arm through Summer's and tugged her toward the bulls waiting patiently in holding pens. "What the hell was that?" I whispered to her.

She looked confused. "What?"

"That flirting? That eye contact? The sparks flying in the air between the two of you?"

She elbowed me sharply. "Shh! Stop it. That wasn't flirting. It was just friendly rivalry. He's practically my brother."

I frowned. "Oh, come off it. You haven't seen the guy in years. He is *not* practically your brother, nor should you want him to be, because he's flipping gorgeous and obviously totally into you."

"Stop! He's not. He knows I have a boyfriend. He met Austin last time he stayed here."

I glanced back over my shoulder at where Dominic was undoing the buttons on his shirt. He kept shooting little glances in Summer's direction.

"Mmm hmm. If you say so."

Summer ignored me, but when she turned around to call out to Dominic, her mouth fell open.

Couldn't blame her. Shirtless Dominic was a thing of beauty. His olive skin gleamed in the sunlight, black and gray tattoos covering his arms and chest. In only a cowboy hat and a pair of Wranglers, he could have stepped right out of a magazine or a Hollywood movie.

"Still got that accountant boyfriend who can't ride and doesn't support your dreams, Summer?" I asked sweetly.

She shot me a dirty look and closed her mouth, busying herself with the bulls. "I know what you're doing."

I raised an eyebrow. "What's that?"

"You're deflecting. You haven't even mentioned your date last night."

My smile fell. "I wasn't deliberately not mentioning it, there's just not much to tell."

Summer shooed a bull into the chute and locked it in place behind him. "So you just went over there for dinner and ate a meal with the man you've been pining over for as long as I've known you?"

I bent to scoop up a rope and threw it across the bull's

back. Then glanced around to see if anyone else was in earshot. Frost, Johnny, and their wives had taken up spots outside the ring to watch. Dominic was laughing at something his dad had said while he hung his shirt over the fence.

"Fine. There was more than just eating."

Summer let out a whoop. "Yes! Was it as amazing as you've been dreaming of?"

The corner of my mouth lifted. "We didn't have sex...but what we did do made me pretty certain it would be better than my daydreams."

"Wow, big praise. So what's the problem?"

My smile fell. "The problem is that Nate doesn't live here anymore. Sure, his mail might go to his old house, but he's never there. So what exactly am I doing with him?"

"Having mind-blowing sex?" Summer said it so simply, as if it were completely obvious.

"Yeah, maybe. But then when he leaves, what am I left with?"

"Sexual satisfaction?"

"And a broken heart."

Summer sighed, eyeing Dominic advancing toward us. "You've had a broken heart all these years anyway. Trust me. Have some fun now while he's here, and while you can. Before you're old and married like I am."

"You're twenty-two and you are not married, Summer Hunt. Nobody is forcing you to stay with Austin."

"I love him."

"Do you?"

Dominic cleared his throat, his hands shoved deep in his pockets, making his jeans even lower on his hips.

Good Lord, Summer had rocks in her head.

"Am I interrupting?" His gaze trailed over Summer's

face, too slowly and with too much concern to be entirely platonic.

Just as I'd suspected.

"No," Summer said too quickly. "We're about ready. Climb up."

Then we were all about getting Dominic on his ride, and there was no further chance to dissect my love life. Or Summer's.

13

HALLIE

I spent the entire afternoon hauling ropes, opening gates, and climbing fences if the bulls got too close. There had been twenty or so cowboys, plus Summer and Dominic who all rode multiple times, before Frost finally called it a day on practice. By then, my arms and shoulders ached, and I was covered head to toe in dirt.

I headed back to my place, desperately looking forward a long soak in a hot bath and an early night.

But when I pulled into my driveway there was a big, sinfully handsome cowboy sitting on my front steps, blocking my entrance.

"What are you doing here?" I smoothed back my hair self-consciously, hoping it wasn't sticking up in weird angles from my hat.

Nate stood and approached with slow, cautious steps like I was a pissed-off bull. "I wanted to check in on you and make sure you really were okay after last night. But I realized I don't even have your phone number anymore."

"I changed it after you left."

He nodded. "I still had your mom's landline, though. She told me you bought this place." His smile relaxed. "It's amazing."

I trudged past him and up the stairs to the front door. "It's a dump. But it will be something when I'm done with it. It's just slow going. I don't have the money to pay someone to renovate it, so I have to do it myself, around my hours at the ranch."

I left the door open behind me, and he followed me inside, gazing around at the entranceway. I couldn't help but smile. His expression was identical to the one I'd worn the day I first saw it, too. This house was ancient, but there was a magic in the high ceilings and ornate staircases. I could so clearly see in my mind how it must have been in its heyday, with gleaming polished floors, overstuffed couches, and hidden nooks where you could tuck yourself away with a book or gaze out the window at the gardens.

It currently had none of those things, but one day...

Nate could see it, too. I could tell.

"You want a tour?" I asked.

He shook his head. "You're exhausted. I actually came to ask if I could take you out. But now maybe I'm asking if I can run you a bath and cook you dinner?"

My heart squeezed. He still knew how to read me. He always knew what I was thinking, or needing, without me even saying it.

Well, except for that one time when I'd fallen in love with him.

He hadn't seen that coming.

There was still the fact he was leaving in a few days, but was I really going to push him away? All it took was one look at his face, and I knew I couldn't. If I only got a few days with him, then I would take it, even knowing he'd break my heart again when he left.

The alternative was breaking my own heart right now. And I just couldn't do it. Not yet, when he was right here, in my home, trying to take care of me, and so sinfully hot doing it. Summer was right on that account. I'd lived with a broken heart all these years; it couldn't be any worse. I might as well make some memories that might get me through the next round of Nate-induced angst. "I've got a claw-foot bathtub. It's big enough for two, if you want to join me?"

He stepped in closer, his fingers brushing over my arms, shooting tingles across my skin. "Is that what you really want? I thought after last night..."

I waved a hand around like last night didn't matter. "I get it, Nate. You have a life, and you're leaving to go back to it. This is just for fun." I grabbed the waistband of his jeans and tugged him closer. "Do you really want to talk about leaving when I'm right here, asking you to get naked with me?"

A slow grin spread across his face. "Well, if you put it that way." He gripped my hips, and in one quick movement, I was slung over his shoulder in a fireman's hold as he stormed up the stairs.

I laughed, dangling down his back. "Left at the top!"

He followed directions, finding the master bathroom with ease and fitting the plug to the drain before turning on the faucet. Water fell from the spout, splashing against the white porcelain, and he added a squirt of the perfumed bubble bath solution I kept on the bathroom shelf.

"This room was the first one I renovated," I told him, watching the water level rise and liquid froth into bubbles.

"Not surprised. You always did love to take baths. Every time I went to your place to pick you up for anything, I'd have to wait an extra thirty minutes because you'd still be soaking."

I smiled at the memory. "Do you still hate them?"

He shrugged. "I don't think I've had one since I left. Our hotel rooms are nice enough, but they aren't fancy. There's normally only a shower."

I pouted at that. "Life on the road doesn't sound all that glamorous."

"It's not. Living out of a suitcase. Eating out every night. Missing people." His gaze collided with mine. "I miss you. All the time."

I closed my eyes, the intensity of his stare too much. "Don't. Please."

He fingered the hem of my T-shirt then lifted it.

I raised my arms so he could remove it before opening my eyes. "Don't say things like that. Not when you have to leave again. It's too hard."

He gave a small sad smile, then nodded. "You're right. I'm sorry."

I put a finger to his lips. "Don't be. It is what it is." I traced it over his chin, then lower to run down his chest and abs until I bunched my fingers into the fabric of his shirt and pushed it up. He helped, pulling it off the rest of the way.

"We still have a few days," I murmured. "Let's just make the most of it." I popped the button on his jeans and undid the zipper of his fly.

He watched me, his gaze growing heated with every second that passed.

"I want to see you," I admitted, tugging his jeans lower.

His breath hitched, but he leaned in, grasping my chin and tilting my face up. He kissed me softly. "I want that, too." His fingers trailed over my bare shoulders to the clasp of my bra. "Can I take this off you?"

I nodded. He was so sweet and respectful. He always had been. It was one of the things I loved about him.

Not that I could tell him.

I busied myself with his jeans again so he wouldn't see the truth in my eyes. My bra fell away, and he cupped my breasts, pinching my nipples in just the way I liked. A spike of pleasure soared through me, and I picked up the pace in getting him naked. We'd been interrupted last night, before I could touch him, and I planned to rectify that now.

I tucked my fingers into the elastic of his boxer briefs and pushed them down his hips. His cock was already half hard, and I ran my hand over it experimentally, watching it stiffen beneath my touch.

He groaned, his dick standing at full mast instantly. I bit my lip. He was big. Bigger than any of the guys I'd been with. I looked up at him and couldn't help but laugh.

He raised an eyebrow. "Wow, Hal. Can't say that's the usual reaction I get when I get naked with a woman. Thanks for putting me in my place."

I laughed. "No, no, your dick is great. Perfect. Super big."

He snorted at that. "But?"

"It's just kinda weird that I'm seeing you naked."

He reached over to turn off the faucet. "You're half naked, too, you know."

"Yeah, but you already saw my boobs last night. I've definitely never seen your...snake."

He cracked up laughing. "My snake?"

"Dick, cock, whatever."

"At least tell me it's an anaconda?"

"Don't flatter yourself."

He caught me around the waist and picked me right off the floor. "You're paying for that!" He scooped my legs up from beneath me and put me down in the bath, still wearing my jeans.

"Nate!" I squealed.

He seemed smugly satisfied with himself.

"Joke's on you, buddy. Do you know how difficult it is to get off wet denim?"

His face fell. "I might have made a grave error."

"Just get in here."

I undid the button on my jeans and lay back, letting the warm water slide over my torso. I closed my eyes for the briefest of moments, just enjoying it, even though my jeans were plastered to my body. But then Nate was out of his boots and sliding into the other end of the bath. He dropped down into the water and immediately tugged at my jeans, too. It was a mammoth effort to get them off, but then we were both naked and staring at each other across a bubble-filled tub.

"Never done this with you before," he said with a grin.

"Nope."

He grabbed my bodywash from the shelf and squeezed a dollop onto his wet palm. "Come here."

I glided through the water to sit between his widespread legs and turned around so my back was to him. He dripped the bodywash across my shoulders then kneaded in in, massaging my aching muscles.

I sank a little in the water, going completely boneless at the sensation. "That feels amazing. Don't stop. Ever. I don't care how cold this bath gets, or how wrinkled and water-logged our skin gets, we're never getting out."

He chuckled, but he didn't disagree. His fingers slid

across my shoulders, and then lower, kneading along my biceps, until I slumped back against his chest, half delirious from how good it felt.

I'd never really had a boyfriend. There'd been a few guys I'd seen more than once or twice, but they had always fizzled out quickly. None of them had ever taken their time with me like this, just touching me because it felt good, without any expectation of anything in return.

None of them had ever cared about me, and that was what felt different here.

Nate cared.

Like he could read my mind, his fingers slipped from the muscles of my arms, across to my breasts, lathering them up with soap. He squeezed them in his big hands, and warmth shot through my body. His fingers clamped around my nipples, rolling them and working them, until I moaned and writhed. He shifted forward and reached lower, skating over my mound to find my clit.

"Oh." My fingers dug into the strong muscles of his thighs clamped around me. His dick was hard at my back, and I tried to reach around to grasp him, but there wasn't enough room.

Nate's mouth lowered to my ear. "Stop wriggling. Let me make you come."

I stubbornly shook my head. He'd already done that once last night. I stood, water sluicing off my body in rivulets, and spun to face him. "It's my t—"

He grabbed my ass and planted his mouth over my pussy, which was right at his eye height, with him sitting and me standing. He moved so quickly, and took me by such surprise, that my legs wobbled and I had to clutch at his head to steady myself. "Nate!"

His tongue speared between my legs, licking over my folds and through my core. The next time I said his name it was more of a breathy moan than a shout.

He lapped at me, taking away the water from the bath and urging me to widen my stance as far as I could. His stubble rasped over the sensitive skin of my inner thighs, only adding to the maddening sensation building within me.

"Put one foot up on the edge," he encouraged me.

I did as I was told, opening myself up fully to him. I ran my fingers through his dark blond hair, half-stroking him, half-holding him to me, because now that he'd started, I couldn't bear for him to stop. He edged his way beneath me, tonguing from my clit, all the way back to my ass. My hips rolled wantonly, as if they had a mind of their own, and he devoured my arousal with every swipe of his tongue.

My legs trembled, and the beginnings of a mind-shattering orgasm rolled in.

But then he stopped, pulling his face from between my legs. I couldn't help the whimper that escaped me.

He stood and stepped from the bath, holding my hand as I did the same. He wrapped a towel around me, then kissed my neck. "Can't let you come yet. I told you, I'm not done."

Not done? What more was there? He'd already got me to the brink of orgasm quicker than I could even do it myself. But the breather made me remember why I'd started all this. I tugged him toward my bedroom, but the hallway was long and it suddenly felt like a million miles. Halfway to my room, I spun to face him and dropped to my knees.

His thick cock jutted out in front of me, and I closed my mouth over him before he could stop me.

I was rewarded with a hiss of pleasure and his fingers spearing into the wet lengths of my hair.

"Fuck, Hallie. I wanted to make you come first."

I ignored him, running my tongue over the ridged underside until he tightened his grip on my hair.

"One hand, Hallie. Use the other between your legs. I want you on the edge."

I moaned around his cock, and his balls tightened at the noise. I did as he said, using my right, dominant, hand to grip his length while I sucked the head of his cock. The other hand fell between my legs to work my clit.

I was so wet. My fingers slipped between my folds without resistance, and I rubbed my bundle of nerves until I was right back where I'd been in the bathtub, orgasm threatening.

I jerked away from his cock. "Nate, I need to come!"

He dragged me to my feet and pushed me up against the wall. His mouth slammed down on mine, his body crushing me. On instinct, I wrapped one leg around his ass, tilting my pelvis so it lined up better with his.

"Nate! Please!"

His dick notched at my entrance and then pushed inside. I screamed out his name again, shattering into a thousand pieces, the orgasm blacking out my vision as blood stormed around my body, taking fireworks of pleasure with it. He withdrew and drove home again, and then again, his dick stretching and filling me so perfectly it was as if we were two pieces of the same puzzle. My internal walls clenched down around him, and he buried his face in my neck.

"God, you're so tight. I've wanted to do this for so long."

He was saying everything I'd ever dreamed of him saying, but words said in the heat of passion didn't mean anything. I knew that. Though it was hard to remember when he'd sounded so sincere.

He slowed his pace, torturing us both. Our gazes collided, and there was something in his eyes I couldn't read. One I'd never seen before, but it pierced me to my very soul and took away my breath. My chest locked up with the thought that this might be the only time I got to do this with him.

Instinctively, I knew there'd never be sex like this again. Because no one else was Nate.

He'd just ruined me for all other men. And he wasn't mine to keep.

I couldn't bear to look at him. I turned around, flattening my palms to the wall.

Nate reached around, finding my clit again with his fingers while he entered me from behind.

We both groaned at the new position, but it was good. A new orgasm dawning distracted me, drawing me out of my head and drowning those thoughts with physical sensation.

That was easier to deal with than the feelings and attachments that were wrapping around my heart.

"Faster, Nate. Harder."

His fingers dug into my hips, holding me in place while he drove into me. His lips pressed to the back of my neck, and when my second orgasm barreled into me, Nate gave a groan of pure ecstasy. I splintered in half, orgasm roaring, while Nate stilled, spilling himself inside.

His bodyweight crushed me, both of us breathing hard.

"You okay?" he asked eventually.

"I'm great." Which was the truth, at least physically. I'd never had multiple orgasms during sex before. Not even close.

Emotionally, I was wrecked. And as he pulled away, I

reminded myself he'd be doing that permanently in just a few days.

Days were all we had left.

14

NATE

Hallie was gone when I woke up the next morning, but I knew she would be. She started work early and woke up before dawn, like so many other people around here did. Just like I always had before I moved away. Being on tour had made me lazy. There was rarely a reason to get up at dawn anymore. I ran most mornings, but why do that at four if you can do it at eight? There were no cows that needed milking or other chores that had to get done when you slept in a hotel and had room service just a phone call away.

I got out of Hallie's bed, hating that I'd turned into a city slicker. I might have ridden bulls by night, but in every other sense, I'd lost my country roots.

I'd lost my home. My family.

Hallie.

Bull riding had given me fame and a paycheck that would set me up for the rest of my life.

But then I thought about how I'd lain awake last night, staring at Hallie's hair splayed out over the pillow like a halo, and I realized it had taken a lot from me, too.

I made the bed neatly, another something my parents had drilled into me, but I'd had no need for while living in a hotel. I tucked in the corners of the sheets, smoothed the cover, and lined the pillows up. Satisfaction rolled through me, which was stupid, considering it was just a bed.

With little else to do, now that Hallie was at work and Molly was being taken care of by Shep's parents, I wandered around Hallie's huge house. She was right about it being a dump. Her bedroom and the bathroom had been renovated beautifully, but the rest of the house was still a work in progress. I checked out all the rooms, finding each one in more and more disrepair.

My fingers itched to get in and get dirty.

But I was expected at the hospital, so I drove myself back to Jasmine's place, which was how I was now thinking of my childhood house. It had really hit home for me when the Shepherd's pointed out they'd stayed there more than I had. They lived in Australia, for fuck's sake. It wasn't like their place was just around the corner, and yet they'd managed to be here more often than me.

I'd basically become homeless without really realizing it. And I didn't like how it felt.

I showered and changed my clothes before heading up to the hospital. There was no need for me to stop at the nurses' station, I knew exactly where Jasmine's room was now. I tapped quietly on the door before letting myself in. "Jas?"

I stopped, realizing she was asleep. But she wasn't alone. Shep's bed had been wheeled in and set up beside her, their mattresses pushed as close together as the bedframes would allow. Shep was propped up slightly, his arm resting on Jasmine's pillow as he smoothed back her hair.

A lump formed in my throat at the tender way he gazed

at my sister, and the gentle touch of his fingers. Jasmine's face was free of lines, and she slept peacefully with her man at her side.

Shep looked up and smiled at me, motioning me to his side.

I shook my head. "I can come back later. I don't want to wake her." I backed up toward the door, suddenly uncomfortable.

But Shep's voice was regular volume as he called me back. "Have you met your sister? She sleeps like she's dead if Molly isn't around. And they gave her some pretty decent painkillers not long ago, so she'll be out for a while. But I'm going stir crazy. Come entertain me."

I took the chair by his bedside, and he shifted away from Jasmine so he was facing me. He winced in pain.

I gritted my teeth. I hated seeing him like this. Bandages everywhere and tubes sticking out of his arms. "Should I get someone?"

He waved me off. "No. They only let me stay here with Jasmine if my pain levels aren't needing too much monitoring, so it's better if I just tough it out. I don't want to be apart from her."

Jealousy hit me in the gut.

"Uh-oh, what's that face for?" Shep studied me curiously. "Spill it."

"It's nothing important."

"If it has to do with Hallie Ryan, then I beg to differ."

I sighed. "Am I that obvious?"

"You look like a lovesick fool. But the good news is, apparently she gets the same look around you, if local gossip is anything to go by. So what's the problem?"

"How long have you got?"

Shep gestured to his hospital bed. "Actually, I got nothing but time and a burning need for information."

I rolled my eyes. "Fine. I slept with her."

"Good?"

"Mind-blowing. But it was more than just good sex. She's... different."

"Because you looooove her." He singsonged it, as if he were ten years old and teasing me on the playground.

The words hit me in the gut. "Yeah, maybe I do."

"Whoa. I was joking. You do?"

I threw my hands up in the air. "I don't know! I've never been in love before, but I know I've always loved Hallie. She was my best friend, and it's been hell these last few years not having her in my life. It's not that I've been unhappy exactly. It's just that ever since I came back, and since Hallie and I started talking again..."

"You realized that you're *happier*."

I nodded. "With her. Here. I know Molly hates me, but that's because she doesn't know me. I made a bed this morning, Shep, and felt more satisfaction in that one task than I have doing anything else in a long time."

"But... There's a but coming, right?"

I shrugged. "This isn't my life anymore. I have a contract, and commitments. Fans. Friends on the tour. It's what I know. It's who I am now. I've changed."

"Nothing to say you can't change back."

I slumped in my chair, the entire situation feeling like a lost cause. "And throw away everything I've worked for? Go back to being the penniless boy from the middle of nowhere? Hell, they'll sue me for breach of contract, which would wipe out my savings. I literally wouldn't have a penny to my name."

"I threw away everything and moved halfway across the

world when I met your sister." He smiled over at her sleeping form. "Haven't regretted it for a second. She blows my mind every day. She's beautiful and kind and caring. Selfless. She loves me and Molly as fiercely as I love them." He reached over and gave me a feeble punch in the arm. "Plus she's dynamite in bed."

"Oh God, Shep. Shut up." I grimaced. "I did not need to hear that about my sister."

"Then get out of this hospital room and go work out things with Hallie or I'll keep going. She does this thing with her tongue—"

I shot out of my chair, throwing him a dirty look on my way to the door. "I'm telling the doctor to get you another head scan. What's wrong with you?"

His laughter followed me all the way down the corridor.

15

HALLIE

I worked the entire day at the ranch with a smile on my face. In my head, I just kept playing the night before over and over, remembering every touch and every look Nate had given me, and committing them to memory so I could relive them once he was gone.

I shook my head, mentally berating myself for going there again. I wasn't doing it. I didn't want to ruin the time we had left by constantly reminding myself it was going to end. Maybe he'd want to do the long-distance thing. It wasn't ideal, but the thought of phone sex was fun. We could FaceTime, and I could fly out to his rodeos sometimes...though that would set back my plans for renovating the bed and breakfast. I hadn't exactly budgeted in flights all around the country. And sometimes, he wasn't even in it. Sometimes he was overseas for months at a time.

I pushed all that away with a sigh. It wasn't the time for thinking about that stuff. I still had two nights left with him, and I wanted to make the most of them.

Five minutes before quitting time, Summer found me brushing down the horse I'd been riding. "Hallie! There you are, I've been searching for you everywhere. I really need your help."

I put the brush down and wiped my hands on the back of my jeans. "Okay, what's up?"

"Someone spray-painted the bulls."

My mouth dropped open. "What? Who the hell would do that? And why?" Irritation prickled up my spine. "It was those *bucking* cowboys, wasn't it? So immature."

Summer cocked her head to one side. "You're really running with the creative swearing, aren't you?"

I shrugged. "I think it's a habit now. And don't think I didn't hear you drop one the other day, too. Let me grab some stuff. How the hell are we going to get spray paint off a bunch of bulls? In the squeeze chute?"

Summer shrugged, flitting around the place and throwing a scrubbing brush in my direction. She didn't seem particularly concerned that her charges had been playing pranks. In fact, she almost seemed like she found it funny. The cowshit fumes must have gone to her head. Frost was going to have a coronary when he found out.

I checked my watch and groaned. I was going to be late getting home. Nate and I hadn't made any plans, but I'd definitely hoped to see him again tonight. Buck those cowboys. If I found out which one it was, I was going to spray him in red paint and lock him in Grave Digger's pen.

Summer linked arms with me and led me to the pens. She pointed to the first one, and I groaned. A huge red P was painted on the animal's hind quarters.

"P?" I asked her. "Were they trying to write their names? Which of them starts with a P?" Anger boiled through my blood. This was such a useless waste of time. I dumped my buckets on the ground and climbed the fence to get a better look at the others. They all had letters on their hides. "P. M. O. R."

Summer pointed to the last pen. "That one has a question mark."

I shook my head. "Idiots."

Summer's grin widened. "Mmm. P. M. O. R. Question mark. You ever play those word games, Hal? You know where you unscramble the letters to make a word?"

I glanced at her, then back at the bulls. I switched the letters around in my head a few times. "Prom?"

She grinned and jumped down off the fence. "Took you long enough." She jerked her head behind me.

I spun around, only to find Nate in a suit, a bunch of flowers in his hands, and a shit-eating grin on his face.

My eyes widened, taking him in. Holy hell. I'd always thought he was hot in Wranglers and T-shirts and beat-up old baseball caps. But Nate in a suit was next-level drool-worthy.

He held the flowers out in my direction. "Wanna go to prom with me, Hallie?"

I burst out laughing. "That was you? You painted Frost's bulls?"

He nodded. "Yeah, so you'd better say yes, otherwise his yellin' will all be for nothing."

I stepped in closer, running my fingers down the silky material of his lapels. "What prom are you asking me to, exactly? Last I checked, we weren't in high school anymore."

"I know. But I wanted a do-over. So seriously, Hallie. Summer has a dress for you in her bedroom. Go do your hair and your makeup, or don't. I don't care. I just wanna take you to prom."

I pushed up onto my toes and kissed him quickly. "I've no idea what you're doing."

"But you like it?"

I gazed into his blue eyes. "Yeah, Nate. I like it."

Abandoning the painted bovines and leaving them for someone else to deal with, I found Summer in her bedroom in the main house. She pounced on me the minute I walked through the door, her fingers gripping my arm. "Did you say yes?"

I shook her off before she did me permanent damage. "Of course." I laughed. "Did you help him?"

She nodded happily. "He found me on my lunch break and told me what he was planning. It's been a bitch trying to keep my mouth shut all afternoon."

"Is that why you sent me down to the back paddocks?"

She shrugged. "That, and the fact there really was a fence down. But who cares about that." She shoved me in the direction of the bathroom. "Take a shower, then come choose a dress. I've got shoes, and jewelry, too."

Ten minutes later, I was wrapped in a fluffy white towel and staring at an array of dresses laid out over Summer's bed. "Where did you even get all these?"

Summer had gone to our prom, but I vividly remember it being under duress. She'd always been more comfortable in jeans, and so was I.

"I have two sisters who both went to multiple proms, plus a mother who has spent her life going to WBRA events with my dad. We have an odd amount of fancy clothes for women who work on a bull riding ranch."

"Well, I'm grateful for it. I got rid of the dress I wore to the last prom Nate took me to." I still kind of regretted that.

But after everything had gone pear-shaped, I couldn't bear to look at it hanging in my closet.

"Did he tell you what he's planned?" Summer thrust a green number at me and turned her back so I could get changed.

"No. He told you?" I asked, quickly pulling on my outfit. "I'm done by the way. What do you think?"

She spun around and let out an ear-piercing wolf whistle. "I think we should all have proms at twenty-two because you fill that dress out way better than I did at seventeen."

I grinned at her as I studied my reflection in the mirror. It was a simple style, very Summer in that respect, with spaghetti straps. It didn't reveal a lot of cleavage, but it had a killer split up one side and showed off the definition in my leg. "I love it."

Summer's gaze rolled over my body, and she made me do a spin for her. "How do you not have a panty line in that? It's skintight."

I grinned. "Not wearing any. I've only got the ugly functional cotton pair I wore at work all day."

She laughed. "I don't think Nate will mind, do you?"

A little thrill ran through me at the thought of telling him. I could picture so clearly what his reaction would be. "No, I don't think he'll mind at all."

16

NATE

"Come on, Frost. How long are you going to give me the cold shoulder for? I said I'll be over first thing in the morning to clean off your bulls."

The older man took a sip of his beer, eyeing me as he swallowed. "You'd better."

He frowned, and I just knew there was more he wanted to say. He'd been my coach for years, and I knew all his tells.

I raised an eyebrow, waiting for it. Frost wasn't the sort of guy you could hurry into saying anything. He only spoke when he needed to and wasn't one for idle chitchat.

"It's nice what you're doing for Hallie. But I'm warning you, she's like one of my own daughters now."

"And if I hurt her you're gonna get your shotgun out?"

That earned me a rare smile. "Maybe. Don't fuck it up. She ain't gonna give you a third chance."

I nodded, taking his advice on board.

We both stood as Summer cleared her throat from the top of the stairs. She focused in on me. "You aren't ready for this," she promised.

I sucked in a deep breath. Because I *was* ready now. I

hadn't been, four years ago, when my head had been full of big dreams I'd thought would make me happy. I hadn't seen what was right under my nose.

Hallie appeared at the top of the stairs. Glowing. Gorgeous. The long dress hugged her figure, her luscious leg peeking from a split in the fabric.

I saw her now. Not just tonight, wearing an outfit I couldn't wait to tear off her. Losing her had made me see what I'd taken for granted.

I wouldn't do that again.

Frost muttered something about death and maiming in my direction, but then Hallie reached the bottom stair, and everything else fell away.

"Hey, again. Like my dress?"

She'd curled her hair and left it hanging loose around her shoulders. I brushed it back, letting my fingers rest at the back of her neck, and drew her in. "I do, but I like what's under it more."

She shivered but then turned her face slightly so her lips brushed my ear. "There's nothing under it."

Oh, sweet baby bulls. I groaned, and Hallie pulled away with a wicked glint in her eye.

"Okay, okay," Summer butted in. "Quit staring at each other like that before you make a baby right here in the living room."

Frost made a sound of disgust, and with a final dirty look in my direction, he stalked off.

Summer shooed us toward the door. "Go. Have your prom night re-do. But, Nate, can you come over in the morning? I could use a few pointers for my ride next weekend. Pretty sure you've ridden the bull I drew."

"Which one?"

"Death Defy."

I tried not to grimace, because that bull was no easy animal to conquer. But I knew this was a big meet for her. Doing well this weekend would put her well on track for WBRA. The new season wasn't far away, and it was about time Summer made it onto the team. "Yeah, I've ridden him. I'll be here in the morning. Be ready. I'm going to push you hard."

She nodded eagerly. "Good. That's what I want." She shot a glare in the direction her dad had disappeared. "I think he's coddling me. I need outside eyes."

I doubted it. I knew Frost wanted Summer to make the pro tour as much as anyone. It more likely came down to Summer being stubborn, pushing herself too hard, and not wanting to take advice from her old man. But I had advice to give, and if she wanted to hear it, I'd be here. "I can't wait to watch you be the first woman on the pro tour."

"From your lips... But go, we're boring Hallie with our shop talk."

I slipped my fingers through Hallie's. "I'll make it up to you."

She raised an eyebrow. "You'd better. I've had enough bull talk for one day."

"Let's go then. Prom awaits."

The low-sinking sun splashed oranges and purples across the sky and bathed Hallie in a gentle glow. It was all I could do to keep my eyes on the road and not just openly stare at her. Instead, I snuck glances at her, my gaze constantly drawn to the bare stretch of thigh the split in her dress showed off.

"So, where exactly is this prom you speak of? Pretty sure

the high school already had theirs, so I'm assuming we aren't crashing their party."

I dragged my eyes back to the road. "Nope. Somewhere a little closer to home." I turned down the street where Hallie lived, and she frowned.

"Prom is at my place?"

"Close your eyes. It'll be better if it's a surprise."

She seemed doubtful, but she closed her eyes anyway.

I pulled the car up in Hallie's driveway and set the brake. "Wait there." I got out and ran around the car to her side and opened the door for her.

"Can I look yet?"

"Nope."

I grabbed her hand and led her up the garden path, letting myself inside. It was a good thing nobody around here bothered to lock their doors. It had meant I'd had free rein at Hallie's place all afternoon.

"Step up. And again," I instructed, putting my hand over her eyes, because we were close to my surprise now, and I didn't want her to get impatient and cheat.

"You smell really good, Nate." She inhaled again. "You wore that cologne to our original prom."

I blinked. Had I? "You remember that?"

"I remember everything about that night. The good, and the bad."

I guided her inside and took in my handywork for a moment. Everything was as I'd left it. I sucked in a deep breath. "There'll only be good tonight. I promise."

I moved my hand away and was rewarded with a shocked inhale of breath. Wide-eyed, Hallie spun around in a circle, taking in everything I'd created.

Hallie's house had a beautiful grand living room on the bottom floor. I imagined one day, she'd fill it with couches, and maybe a table for playing board games, or a fireplace to curl up by. But right now, it had been a dumping ground for her tools and supplies. I'd moved them all to a small room around the corner, where they were still easily accessible but not on display for everyone to see. I'd swept the floors and the cobwebs and replaced them with fairy lights, strung from the ceiling. Candles were perched carefully on each step of the staircase that swept up to the second floor, and a table with a white covering sat in the middle of the room. I'd picked flowers from Jasmine's garden for the centerpiece, and I'd left soft music playing while I was gone. Now, I picked up a lighter and lit all the candles one by one, and the effect was complete.

I raised an eyebrow in Hallie's direction. "Well?"

"This is way nicer than our prom was. Where are the tacky streamers and cheap decorations?"

I put a palm on her lower back and guided her to the table. "This is the grown-up version. I did spike the punch, though."

"Trying to get your date drunk?"

I dragged out her chair for her, and when she sat, I kissed the side of the neck. "I have better ways of enticing you to my bed." My kisses turned open-mouthed, and I flicked my tongue over her skin, enjoying the way she shivered.

My dick kicked behind my fly, and I pulled back to get myself under control. I didn't know how I'd ever thought of this woman as just my friend. I had to suck in a deep breath on my way to the kitchen and give my cock a stern talking to about behaving. At least long enough to show Hallie I was serious about redoing our prom night. This wasn't just a ploy to get her into bed. Though I did want that to happen, too. But I wanted to show her I was past the friendship stage.

She deserved an epic romance, and I wanted to be the one who gave it to her.

From the kitchen I grabbed my spiked punch, as well as a tray of finger foods I'd bought for the occasion. I carried it all carefully out, with Hallie watching me with interest.

She laughed as I put it down on the table. "Okay, this is definitely more like what I remember from our prom. I love these mini quiches!"

I dragged the other chair around the circular table so I could sit next to her. "I could have made us a proper meal, but I remember how many of those you ate on prom night. I know they're your favorites."

She shoved one in her mouth and closed her eyes as she happily chewed. "You're my favorite right now. I never make this stuff just for myself."

When she was done picking at the food and sampling the highly alcoholic punch, she smiled at me. "So what time does the bus pick you up on Friday?"

I winced at the reminder. "Nope. Not talking about bull riding tonight."

"I thought this was prom redo? From memory, all we talked about at our original prom was bull riding."

I thought back to that night four years ago and realized she was right. I'd been so amped about being picked for the tour that I'd spent the entire night running my mouth about it to anyone who'd listen. Hallie had been right by my side, completely thrilled for me. She'd been proud.

I'd ruined her prom night by making it all about me.

I wasn't doing that again. Tonight would be all about her.

I put my hand on her knee and squeezed it. "I was such a dickhead, wasn't I? I'm sorry."

She squinted, her head tilted to one side. "You weren't a

dickhead. A huge, exciting thing happened to you. Of course that was going to dominate our conversation."

"I hate I wasn't here for your big exciting things."

She laughed. "There's nothing big or exciting here."

"Are you kidding? You bought a house, Hallie. Not even a house, really, because this place is huge. What are you going to do with it?"

She lifted a shoulder. "Restore it. Turn it back into the B&B it once was. Probably go broke because this isn't exactly a tourist town."

"You don't want to keep working at the ranch?"

"I love it there, don't get me wrong. But the ranch is someone else's dream. This place is mine. So if I open the doors, and nobody comes, then at least I've tried."

I nodded slowly. "Can I ask you something?"

She balled up her napkin and then sat back, her gaze focused on me. "Sure. Anything."

"If you tried and it wasn't everything you hoped it would be, what would you do then?"

She mused on that for a moment. "I guess I'd stop. Regroup. Work out what was causing the problem, then fix it." Her forehead furrowed into a frown. "Are you talking about bull riding?"

"I guess so."

Hallie reared back an inch. "Nate, bull riding is your dream. It always has been. And you're amazing at it. It's not something you can do until you're eighty, so you have to do it now, while you still have the fitness. There are so many people who'd kill to be in your position. Summer for one."

She was right, and I realized exactly how ungrateful I sounded. I'd been given the opportunity of a lifetime. It was something my dad and I had talked about for years before he died. All he'd ever wanted to do was see me make the pros, and he hadn't lived long enough to watch me do it. That was something I'd always regret. I'd been given an opportunity to travel the world, on someone else's dime, and I was sitting here whining about it when Hallie had never even left the state.

"Do you want to dance?" I asked, changing the subject.

The frown smoothed out, and she put her hand in mine.

I pulled her up, and we came together right as the song changed. It was a random playlist I'd found online, and I didn't recognize the song, but it was slow and sexy and the perfect distraction from my career woes. Hallie wrapped her arms around my neck, and I tugged her close, breathing her in. We swayed together, her head resting on my shoulder, while I committed her body to memory. I smoothed my palms down her back and over the curve of her perfect ass, cupping her cheeks and squeezing them.

She laughed, her lips against my neck. "You didn't do that last prom." She paused for a moment, then reared back slightly to look me in the eye. "I wanted you to, though."

My fingers roamed back to her hips and over the sides of her thighs. One slid over silky material, while the other grazed her bare flesh, reminding me of what she'd said earlier about not wearing anything underneath. "What else did you want me to do?"

Her cheeks went pink.

"I'm making you blush again."

"You do that a lot."

"I know, and I like it. Tell me, Hallie. What did you want me to do that night? I want to know everything you were dreaming or hoping for. Because I want to make them all happen."

Her cheeks blazed. "Stop, I can't. It's too humiliating."

I stopped dancing. "Humiliating? Hallie, fuck. Don't you

know how much I want you? I'm not that same boy I once was. And I know you've changed, too. We're running on borrowed time here, we both know that, but I want to give you everything you missed out on."

She swallowed hard, but she still didn't say anything.

I hauled her back in by her hips, so close that she couldn't look me in the face anymore. It was easier to tell someone what you wanted when you weren't staring directly at them. "I can't tell you I was hoping for anything that night. But every night since, I've wished I could be here, right as we are now. Every single night, I've regretted not holding you like this. I regret not tipping your chin up and kissing your lips in front of everyone."

My lips found her neck and worked their way along her jaw until her lips met mine. I closed my eyes as our mouths touched, falling into the kiss, and putting into it everything I'd lost in the past four years, everything I still wanted to give her. We kissed like it was the first time and the last time, all rolled into one. But it was neither; because I knew in that moment I couldn't let Hallie go again. Even when I got back on that bus on Friday morning and watched it pull away from her. There'd be no one else like her. I already knew it. I'd spent four years trying to find someone, but it always came back to her.

But there was no room in my life for relationships, even one I wanted badly. That was all I could think of, ever since I'd talked to Shep at the hospital. I'd be on tour until I was injured, or just not good enough anymore. Some of the guys rode until they were thirty-five. That was still thirteen years away for me. What the hell was Hallie supposed to do all that time? Sit at home and wait for me? When at best, I was home for a few days twice a year? What kind of life was that?

Not one I wanted for her.

And she couldn't come with me. Her B&B wasn't exactly a portable idea.

I had to love her enough to let her go. Even if it would kill me in the process.

17

HALLIE

Nate's words ripped through my chest, opening up old wounds and creating new ones. He was saying everything I'd wanted him to say, and more, but all with the knowledge that this feeling was temporary.

Due to expire.

Ending.

His lips trailed to my ear. "If I'd been smarter back then, I would have got you alone. In a dark corner." His fingers crept up the split in my dress, and when he got to the top, he yanked the slinky fabric up, exposing the bare skin of my hip.

My breath hitched, his palm sliding beneath my dress, reaching around to cup my naked ass.

"I would have kissed you. Distracted you with my tongue while my hands touched you here." He squeezed my ass then slipped around the front to cup my mound. "And here."

On instinct, my stance widened, encouraging his touch at my core.

His voice was barely more than a murmur in my ear as his finger nudged my clit. "All our friends would have been dancing on the dance floor, drinking punch, and taking photos, while I had my fingers inside you."

His fingers slid through my building wetness, and he fit one up inside me. My eyes closed at the sensation, and I bunched my fingers in his fitted shirt.

He pumped in and out a few times, moving back to touch my clit before plunging in again. I held him tighter, whimpering at the sensation.

"You like it when I touch you here, Hallie?"

I whimpered louder, rolling my hips. My dress was hitched up and to the side, exposing my pussy, so it was a good thing we weren't really in a room full of people, but the imagery he conjured up with his dirty words had me so hot. My nipples beaded, and I was suddenly dying to be naked with him. "I like it when you touch me everywhere."

His tongue trailed up my neck, tasting me. He found the zipper on the back of my dress and lowered it. He kissed my shoulder, pushing off the straps so the material pooled around my middle. Then he dragged it lower, until it fell away from my hips and down my legs, puddling on the floor around my heels.

He'd left me completely bare and on show for him.

His fiery gaze stroked me from head to toe. The blush that hadn't disappeared since he'd started telling me what he wanted to do to me spread down my neck and across my chest, my stomach, my limbs. It took with it a burning heat that boiled my blood and made the nerve endings between my legs ache with need.

He was completely dressed, and I was completely naked. There was something so incredibly hot about that. He stepped in and dipped his head to suck one nipple into his mouth. I cried out at his touch, the heat, the wetness, and speared my fingers into his hair. He nipped at me, driving me higher, squeezing my other nipple with his fingers.

I needed more. More than his mouth and his fingers. I needed all of him. I grabbed at the waistband of his suit pants, undoing the button and zipper as quickly as I could. I shoved his pants and underwear down his legs, freeing his impressive erection.

He was thick and hard. His white button-down shirt hung long, brushing the tops of his thighs. I attacked it with nimble fingers, undoing the buttons and pulling the material aside, taking in each ripple of his abs and the firmness of his pecs. He went to push it off his arms, but he was so sexy just standing there, chest, abs, and cock visible beneath his open white shirt. I shoved him back toward one of the chairs, and he sat with a knowing smirk.

"You gonna ride me, Hallie? You want me to be your bull?"

I straddled him, lining his dick up with my entrance, but not sinking down onto it. His cockhead slipped through the wetness between my lower lips, and he hissed out his agony.

"Fuck. You're so wet. I want in."

I teased him some more, just like he'd done to me, kissing his neck while his erection bobbed between my legs, getting close to the goal, but never more than nudging against my clit. I ached so bad to be filled, but I wanted him right there with me. I stroked him a few times with my hands, pumping him up and down and taking just the head of him inside me.

"Oh," I moaned, my legs wobbling. I wanted more. I wanted everything, and there was no way I could keep this up, no matter how much I was enjoying it.

I didn't have to.

Nate gripped my hips and caught my attention with a

blazing look. “I’m gonna fuck you, Hallie. Hard and fast, unless you tell me not to.”

Pleasure spiked in my core at his promise. I sank down onto his cock, impaling myself fully on his thick, hard length. I screamed his name as he stretched me, and his shouts echoed around the room. I recovered enough to find a rhythm, rocking my hips over him, while his fingers punished my hips. He held me so tightly, guiding my movements, thrusting up into me, our thighs slapping together.

I wrapped my arms around his shoulders, kissing him passionately, our tongues sliding and moving together, searching and wanting. A greedy need for him took over me while I ground against him, chasing my orgasm.

I wanted Nate. Not just for tonight.

There was more here than a fling. My heart swelled along with building orgasm, and just like the last time we’d done this, we switched from straight-up fucking to something more. Our pace slowed. He stared into my eyes and held me just that little bit closer.

“Hallie,” he murmured.

To my horror, I found there was a lump in my throat. I tried to swallow it down, but it stubbornly refused to budge.

This man was going to leave me.

Right after I’d fallen in love with him.

I slammed my eyes closed, unable to face him anymore, and tried to bury the moment in the physical. “I’m close,” I moaned, picking up the pace again.

Nate stilled for a moment, but I didn’t dare look at him. I couldn’t. It was too hard. Mentally, I begged him not to push. I didn’t want to be the girl who embarrassed herself not only at her high school prom, but at her prom do-over.

Crying in the middle of sex would most definitely be embarrassing.

Whether Nate knew what I was feeling or not, I didn't know. But he took my verbal cues and reached a hand between us, finding my clit.

It was good, his fingers working me there, while his dick filled my core. I moved faster, harder, fighting to lose myself in the orgasm funneling down on me. I threw my head back as the pressure reached boiling point, and with a final hard thrust inside me, Nate threw me off the edge of the cliff and sent me spiraling into oblivion.

An oblivion where I didn't have to think about or feel the agony of him leaving me.

Again.

18

NATE

"Get your arm up higher. If you don't qualify because you touched that damn bull, I will literally hunt you down and take off your arm myself!"

The buzzer sounded, and Summer jumped off the back off her bull, landing easily on her feet and sprinted for the fence. She shot me a dirty look from across the other side of the ring. "I'm regretting asking for your help. You're a worse nag than my dad."

I grinned. "Did you forget who trained me?"

She grumbled under her breath, but when I jerked my head toward the bucking chutes, she pulled her hat lower on her brow and strode off. I could see her lips moving as she mumbled to herself, and her left hand rose into the air while she talked her way through the ride in her mind.

Frost had taught her that. Just like he'd taught me. She was ready. She was going to kill it at the rodeo on Saturday. I was just bummed I wouldn't be here to see it.

Hallie was acting as Summer's rope man, and Dominic was on the gates. I'd met Dominic once or twice when we'd been kids, and he'd come out here to ride during the summer. But I'd barely recognized the guy now. He was as tall as I was, and just as broad, but where I was blond, he was dark. Since I'd last seen him, he'd acquired a bunch of intricate tattoos that curled out from beneath his rolled-up shirtsleeves and up the side of his neck.

I shot a glance at Summer's boyfriend, Austin, sitting on the seats behind the chute. The guy hadn't even glanced up from his phone once since I'd arrived. I had no idea what he was even doing here. It was clear he had no interest in watching Summer ride.

Frost appeared from the house and took up a place by my side, just as Summer's bull burst from the gate.

"Get your arm up!" Frost and I yelled in unison.

He chuckled, but then his mouth flattened out into a worried frown. "Something's come up. You know Dominic's old man?"

"Johnny?"

"Yeah. He's got some bulls he wants me to go inspect with him in Wyoming."

"So go."

"Summer has a rodeo this weekend."

I peered at him from under my hat. "Yeah, so? She's twenty-two, Frost. Not twelve. She can get herself to a rodeo."

He shoved his hands in his pockets. "She needs to ride well this weekend if she's going to have enough points to qualify. There's only a couple more rounds left. I'd feel a whole lot better about leaving if you were gonna be there with her."

I shook my head. "You know I would if I could. But the bus picks me up tomorrow morning. I'll be in Texas by the time she rides."

He took his hat off and ran a hand through his short

blond hair. He had a few more grays since I'd left, and I'd bet most of them were caused by his headstrong eldest daughter.

Done with her ride, Summer ran for the fence and caught the end of our conversation. "Don't be ridiculous, Dad. Go to Wyoming. I'll be fine for one rodeo without you."

Dominic lifted his head. "I can go with her."

Summer frowned at him. "I don't need an escort."

"Never said I wanted to be your escort. I just meant as a friend. Not as your coach. I want to watch you ride."

Summer gazed down at her feet. "Oh. Sorry. Yeah, sure. You can drive down with us."

"Us?"

"Me. Austin. Hallie, you coming, too?"

Hallie grinned from the top of the chute. "Wouldn't miss it."

A pang of jealousy lit up my chest. The four of them would be making the two-hour trip together. Probably staying at a hotel that night. I eyed Dominic again. Sure, he was all up in Summer's grill right now, with his gaze lingering on her long after he thought anyone was watching. But she was loyal to a fault, and she was with Austin. It wouldn't take Dominic long to refocus on the only other single woman in the car.

I swallowed thickly and turned to Frost so Hallie wouldn't see the expression on my face. I wanted her to be happy. I had no right getting jealous. "Seems like Summer has it covered. Go get on a plane. Take a few extra days off while you're at it, maybe? You look like you need a break."

Frost narrowed his eyes at me. "And you look like you've got a smart mouth."

"Fine. I'm just saying, she's not your little girl anymore. You can go to Wyoming for a weekend."

Frost watched with his lip curled in disgust as Summer walked over to Austin and sat herself in his lap. She wasn't the only one watching. Dominic looked like the scene was ripping him in two.

Frost huffed out a sigh. "You just wait till you have kids of your own one day. She's always going to be my little girl." With that he stomped off into the house again.

I glanced over at Hallie, who had fallen into conversation with Dominic to avoid the awkwardness of standing there watching Summer and Austin make out. I'd never thought about having kids of my own, not until I'd had to take care of Molly for a few days. The idea of settling down with kids and a family had always felt light-years away.

But that was before I came back home. That was before Hallie. Now, the idea of kids and roots didn't seem quite so terrifying.

In fact, it sounded kinda nice.

She laughed at something Dominic said, her eyes crinkling in the corners in a true smile.

It would be somebody else who got to do all those things with her. Somebody she met at the bar on a Friday night. Or someone who came to stay at her B&B on a work trip and fell head over heels for the small-town girl.

Someone who wasn't me. I couldn't ask her to wait. I couldn't ask her to come with me. There was no future there.

Just one last night, where I would pretend tomorrow didn't exist.

19

HALLIE

Nate wanted to spend some time with his sister and brother-in-law before he left, but when he asked if I'd come, too, I couldn't agree quick enough.

He drove me to the hospital on his bike, tucked to his back, arms tight around his middle. When we got off, he linked his fingers through mine, but we walked silently along the halls and up the stairs to Jasmine and Shep's room.

He knocked, then opened the door for us, and I poked my head in tentatively, not exactly sure what to expect. Nate had told me they were doing better, but the images of them slumped in their overturned car, cut and bleeding, were still firmly ingrained in my memory. Those scenes were something I would never forget, I knew that.

It was a relief to fill my head with the image in front of me now. The two of them were still clearly hurting, with casts, bandages, and machines attached to them, but Shep was sitting up in his bed, and Jasmine was reclining in an armchair next to him. I let myself drink in the sight of them smiling, happy, no blood gushing down their faces, or concern that they might not be breathing. They were very much alive and on the mend.

A lump rose in my throat, and I gave Jasmine a watery smile. "You look so much better."

She patted the seat next to her, and I let go of Nate's hand to sit by her side. She squeezed my arm. "I'm glad you're here. I wanted to thank you. For what you did for Molly after the crash."

"I'm just glad I could help. And that you're all okay."

"We got lucky. But you went above and beyond, and I won't forget it."

I tried to smile, but it was uncomfortable to take in her praises. I'd only done what anybody would have. Okay, maybe most people wouldn't have stayed at the hospital all night, making sure their baby was okay, but Molly was a little piece of Nate, too, and that wasn't easy to walk away from.

I glanced over at him, deep in conversation with Shep. I needed to start mentally distancing myself from him, so I could physically distance myself from him in the morning. But it was so hard, when every time I looked at him, my brain screamed, "He's it!"

Jasmine touched my arm. "Will you come for a stroll with me? Just down the hall. There's some…" She shot a glance at her brother who was frowning at her. "Some feminine products I need."

I stood quickly. "I can get them for you."

But Jasmine pushed herself from the chair, gathering up a pair of crutches leaning against the wall. "No, I need the practice."

When Nate started to argue, she gave him a stern, older sister glare. "Doctor's orders."

I walked slowly while Jasmine swung her heavy cast

awkwardly, limping our way out of the room and down the corridor. She stopped for a breather just a few feet from the door.

"Are you okay?" I peered around for someone to help, but we were still yards from the nurses' station.

Jasmine waved her hand. "Fine. Fine. But I don't really need any feminine products. I just wanted to talk to you alone."

"Oh." I pointed at a set of hard plastic chairs bolted to the floor. "Maybe we should sit."

"Before I fall, preferably."

I cringed and moved a little closer to her, hovering as if she'd tumble at any moment. She sank into the seats with a groan, completely out of breath from the short walk.

"What did you want to talk to me about?" I was suddenly nervous, like I'd been sent to the principal's office. Or like I was meeting my boyfriend's mother for the first time. Jasmine had the slightly intimidating authority figure stare down pat.

"You're in love with my brother, aren't you?"

Breath whooshed out of me on a sharp exhale, and I opened my mouth to deny it. I could barely admit it to myself, let alone say it out loud. People didn't fall in love in a matter of days. Which meant I'd been in love with Nate since we were teenagers. And I hadn't stopped loving him all these years, despite the fact we hadn't seen or spoken to each other once. That was possibly the most pathetic thing I'd ever heard. I liked Jasmine. Respected her. She had a wonderful job here at the hospital, and a man who loved her. A beautiful child. In comparison, I was a stupid kid with a killer crush, and a case of puppy love I just couldn't get over.

Jasmine held up a hand to stop my protests. "There's no

point denying it. I can see that you are. You have that same expression on your face that I had when I first met Shep."

I gazed down at my hands. "How long did it take you to fall in love with him?"

She thought that over for a moment, a smile tugging at her lips. "About three minutes. He's got that adorable accent, and even though he had a raging case of appendicitis, he still managed to charm the pants off me. Quite literally. He had me naked approximately five minutes after he'd checked himself out and was no longer my patient."

We both smiled at that, but then she picked up my hand and squeezed it. "The point is, I know what it looks like to love someone. You need to tell him."

"I can't. He's going back on the road tomorrow."

"What if he didn't?"

I couldn't even fathom that thought. "That's exactly why I can't say anything. I can't tell him I love him or ask him to stay. He's too good for that. Frost always talks about how Nate's going to be world champion before he's twenty-five."

Jasmine frowned. "Or he'll fall off a bull and get stabbed through the liver with a horn. Or he'll blow out his knee or his shoulder. Or he'll end up with one too many concussions, and the doctors will rule him out permanently."

There was fear in her voice. It was the same fear I had whenever he rode. "He can't not go because we're scared he'll get hurt."

She sighed. "I know. And I would never ask that of him. But right now, he has no reason to stay. No reason to change his mind and consider another path. One that might just make him happier than the one he's on now. So what I'm saying is, maybe you should give him one. Give him the option, Hallie. He needs all the information. If he chooses his career, then that's fine. But right now, he doesn't see there could be another way to being happy. Because you aren't telling him how you feel."

She didn't give me a chance to respond. She just grabbed her crutches and limped back to her room, while I sat and stared after her like I'd been slapped in the face with a fish.

20

NATE

When Jasmine returned alone, I raised an eyebrow of concern in her direction. "Where's Hallie?"

"She just needed a minute. You can collect her on your way out."

I shot a glance at the doorway, and out into the corridor, but I couldn't see her. "Is she okay?"

Jasmine put her arms around my middle and squeezed. "She's fine. But don't leave her waiting. You don't have much longer before you have to leave. I'm gonna miss you, little brother. Don't be such a stranger, huh? There's good things in this town."

"Like me," Shep called from his bed. "And the steak at the bar. You can't tell me you get steak like that anywhere else. You know that feeling you get when you cut into it and how it practically melts on your tongue? Even if you don't come back for me, you should come back for that."

I shook his hand with a grin. "I'll keep that in mind. Take care of my sister, and my niece, okay? No more nearly dying. You don't get to do that twice without an ass-kicking."

He grinned. “Ride hard. We’ll be watching.” He gestured at his banged-up body. “And not only because I’ve got nothing better to do right now.”

My phone rang in my pocket, and it was just as well. I gave my sister and brother-in-law a final wave and headed for the door, pulling my phone out as I went. I swallowed down a lump in my throat. If I’d stayed there in that room a moment longer, I might have cried on them like a complete pussy. What the fuck was wrong with me? I’d said these goodbyes many a time and never gotten emotional about it.

But something felt different this time.

I didn’t want to leave them. Shep and Jasmine and Molly needed me.

Then there was Hallie. When I thought about leaving her tomorrow, a piercing pain stabbed through my chest. It hurt so bad I couldn’t stand it, so I’d actively forced myself to stop thinking about it.

I glanced at the phone screen and blinked at it in surprise. “Brad?”

“Yeah, kid. It’s me.”

Nerves trickled through me. Brad Pruitt was the head of the WBRA. He didn’t often call me, and when he did, it wasn’t generally for anything good. I spotted Hallie at the other end of the corridor and moved in her direction while I clutched the phone to my ear.

Hallie stood as she saw me and held a hand out when I reached her.

I linked my fingers through hers, reassured by her warmth and touch. “Sorry,” I mouthed to her. “Work.”

She nodded, and we strolled to toward the elevators.

“What’s up that couldn’t wait until tomorrow?” I asked Brad.

“You haven’t heard the news then?”

"World news or bull riding news? Been kinda busy so I haven't really been keeping up with either to be honest."

"Jorge Kinsaya just pulled out of the competition."

I froze. "What? Why?"

Jorge was a hotshot from Brazil, who had dominated the competition for the past five years. None of us had even come close to touching him on the scoreboard.

"Wrecked his ACL on a practice ride yesterday. Isn't that great?"

I frowned at Brad's callous words, though this was nothing new, coming from him. The man liked his riders to win, he always had. And he was cutthroat about getting them, and in turn, himself, the glory. "No, not really. Is he okay?"

"He's completely done until he recovers from surgery. Which puts him out until the new season, thus opening a path for you."

Shit. He was right. No matter how bad I felt for Jorge, him being out of the competition left it wide open for the rest of us. I was clustered in a group that had been well below Jorge's rank, but with him gone, it was anybody's title to take. A flicker of excitement lit up in my chest.

"This is your chance to make your mark, and it couldn't have come at a better time. We're going to hit the ground running once we pick you up tomorrow. We've got a heap of press booked, and even that *Today* show wants to talk to you."

I blinked. "What? Since when does the mainstream media care about bull riders?"

"Since I spun them your story and told them you were in prime position to be our next superstar."

A little thrill of pride shot through all the overwhelm. I might not have particularly liked Brad as a person, but he knew bulls. He knew cowboys. And if he said I had a shot, then hell, maybe I did?

"Sleep well tonight, kid. Tomorrow starts a whole new phase in your career. Be ready for it."

He hung up before I could even say goodbye.

"Something happen?" Hallie asked, as we stepped onto the elevator.

I looked down at her and felt that same familiar tug that happened every time I thought about leaving her. The doors slid shut, and the elevator lurched to life, dropping down a floor. "Yeah, that was my boss—"

A screeching sound pierced the air, right as the elevator slammed to a halt and plunged us into complete darkness.

21

HALLIE

Completely blind, I fell back against the mirrored walls of the elevator, grasping for something to hold on to, with my heart slamming against my ribcage.

"Fuck," Nate swore into the darkness. "Are you okay?"

Apart from nearly having an instant heart attack? "Yeah, I'm fine. Are we stuck?"

The control panel randomly lit up every button with a green glow that cast an eerie light around the small space, before going dark again. But it was enough for Nate to locate the intercom to call for assistance.

"Hello?" Nate asked the crackle that came down the line.

A gruff, bored-sounding voice answered, identifying himself as building maintenance.

"We seem to be stuck in the elevator."

There was a string of muttered curse words. "How many people you got in there with you?"

"Just the two of us."

The guy sighed. "Either of you claustrophobic?"

I didn't like the sound of that. "I'm not exactly thrilled by the idea of being in here, but I'm not claustrophobic."

"Me neither," Nate confirmed.

"Good. Because you're going to be in there for a while. Probably a couple of hours."

"Hours!" Nate and I yelped in unison.

"Yeah, sorry folks. This happened last week, too. I need to get the elevator company out. This isn't something building maintenance can fix."

I slid down the wall to sit on the floor. "Well, that's just great."

Nate sat beside me. "Could be worse."

"How? This is your last night here, and we're spending it stuck in an elevator that smells of fake lemon and bleach."

Nate's head clunked back against the mirror. "You have a point. I had plans for tonight, too."

"Yeah? Like what?"

"I wanted to take you to this spot out on the lake. I was going to feed you, then convince you to go skinny-dipping with me."

I smiled into the darkness. "It wouldn't have taken much convincing."

"Yeah?"

I shrugged even though he wouldn't see it. "Watching you get your gear off is kind of my idea of a good time, you know."

"Right back at ya."

The intercom crackled with static. "Sorry, folks. The repair company is on their way, but like I said, it's not going to be quick. They have to come from Masonville. Don't freak out, though, those elevators aren't airtight, so you'll still be able to breathe."

"Well, that's reassuring," Nate muttered sarcastically.

But my chest tightened at the thought of being in here

for an extended period of time. "Tell me more about this night you had planned. Out on the lake, in the fresh air."

Nate pressed his fingers into my thigh. "Are you okay?"

I shook my head. Then changed my mind and nodded. "I am, as long as I don't think about being in here. Distract me."

Nate's voice sounded slightly huskier when he answered. "I can do that." His fingers traced a path up my thigh.

Even through my jeans, it felt delicious, and was exactly what I needed. His fingers massaging into the tight muscle drew my attention away from the fact we were stuck in a tiny metal box and unlikely to escape any time soon.

"I would have started just like this." He leaned in and kissed the side of my neck. "And then like this." His kisses trailed up my neck, to the sensitive spot by my ear. They turned open-mouthed, sucking, and biting, until my head fell to the side and I closed my eyes.

I gave in to the sensation. Every kiss had me a little less worried about our predicament, both the elevator, and the fact his bus would be here at nine tomorrow morning. When he tilted my face to claim my lips, and his tongue plunged inside my mouth, I forgot entirely.

"Then I would have pulled you to your feet..." He stood, hauling me up by my hands and wrapping his arms around me. "Then kissed you some more."

His kisses were long, and slow, drugging kisses that made me weak at the knees. And wet between my thighs.

"Then I would have undone these buttons..." His fingers slipped the buttons on my shirt from their holes, and he kissed his way down across my collarbone and the swell of my breasts. He pushed my shirt off my shoulder and bit me there, not hard enough to hurt, but plenty hard enough to send a jolt through my system. It woke my entire body up and I realized what we were doing.

"Nate, we're in an elevator!"

He bared my other shoulder and nipped his way across to it, shoving my shirt down my arms with his palms, leaving me in just my jeans and a bra.

"We're at the lake," he mumbled against my skin.

"Nate..."

He chuckled. "Fine. We're in an elevator, but we're stuck here in blackness, for God knows how long. You wanted me to distract you, so that's what I'm doing."

"And if someone walks in?"

He licked his way down between my boobs and cupped them both through my bra. "Isn't that half the fun? That we could get caught?"

My core throbbed. "Keep talking."

"I want to get you naked, knowing the repair guys could get here at any moment."

"What if there's a camera?"

"It's zero visibility in here. Ain't nobody seeing you naked but me, Hallie." He practically growled the last part. "And I want you."

His tongue plunged inside my mouth again, and I dug my fingers into his biceps to keep myself upright. I wanted him, too. So bad. And the thought of doing this with him, in a public place, was something I'd thought about for years. This was his last night. My last chance to be wild and crazy with him. He'd be back out on the road tomorrow, and then I'd have nothing but my memories of him. Did I want a memory of sitting in an elevator shaft, panicking about dying? Or did I want this memory to be of me and him, completely naked in the dark, our bodies joining, and him blowing my mind?

There was no contest.

I grabbed his shirt and yanked it over his head. In a frantic rush he undid my jeans, yanking them down my legs, while I wriggled out of my bra. His jeans were next, until we stood naked in the darkness, both of us breathing hard, as if we'd just run a marathon.

"Quick," I said, lunging for his cock.

But he caught my hand and walked me backward until I hit the mirrors. The cool, smooth surface was a shock against my bare skin, but then Nate followed me in, putting his warm body to my front, his hot, thick erection between us.

"Not having a quickie with you, babe. I want to make you writhe, while you're thinking about someone walking in here and catching us. I want you so lost to the orgasm that you don't even care. I want to get you there." His hand slipped between my legs.

"Oh God," I whispered.

His first touch of my clit had me groaning. He rubbed me slowly, like he had all the time in the world, pinching and squeezing the tiny bundle of nerves until sensation built at the base of my spine. I closed my eyes and leaned my head onto his chest, widening my stance.

His fingers found my opening, wet and needy, and he wasted no more time thrusting two up inside me. Crooking them so he'd hit my G-spot, he worked me until I was trembling and panting.

He dropped to the floor, lifting one of my knees over his shoulder, opening me up to him fully. His mouth landed on my clit, pressing sexy, dirty, open-mouthed kisses between my folds and licking his way up inside me.

I moaned loudly, my nipples beading. I let go of him to cup my breasts, squeezing my nipples between my thumbs and forefingers, rolling them in time with the way I rolled my hips against Nate's tongue. "Nate," I groaned. "Fuck me. Please."

Right on the edge, he stood and pressed his erection to my core, slamming up inside me. I shuddered with desire. I needed him hard and fast, but he was true to his word, slowing the pace and gliding into me like this was a Sunday stroll and not a quick and dirty screw in a public place.

In that moment, it felt like we did have nothing but time. Everything else fell away, and it was just me, held by the man I loved, as he took my mouth with his own and worshipped my body in the way only he knew how.

Tiny whimpers of ecstasy fell from my mouth that quickly turned into cries and pleading.

"I know what you need, Hallie. Let me give it to you."

His fingers reached between us, finding my clit, and that was it. Pleasure spiraled out from the base of my spine, spreading through my body and culminating inside my core. I screamed out my release, muffling it with my mouth fitted against Nate's collarbone, while he pistoned his hips, screwing me so perfectly and so thoroughly that I knew in that moment, he'd ruined me for all other men.

There was no one else. There never would be. It was me and him. And if I couldn't have him, then that was all there was for me.

Jasmine's words urged me on, but it was my heart that opened, finally breaking down the last of the walls I'd erected that night after prom.

"I love you, Nate," I whispered as he came inside me. "I love you so much."

Silently in my head, I added, "*And I know it's selfish, but I don't want you to go.*"

He groaned, stilling inside me, and then freezing, as if he'd only just registered the enormity of my words.

I held my breath.

Then he kissed me. A deep, soul-searing kiss I felt right to my toes. A kiss that spoke volumes to my wide-open heart, encouraging it, filling it with hope.

But when he pulled away, he didn't say a word.

He didn't say it back.

He didn't say he would stay.

22

HALLIE

Nate and I were both fully dressed and quiet when we were rescued from the elevator. It was a relief to finally be out of the dark, but in the cold light that flooded the elevator, my whispered words of love that he hadn't returned hung in the air between us.

We rode back to his place, where I'd left my car, and I hovered, unsure whether I should stay or go.

He answered that unspoken question by leading me to his bedroom, stripping me of my clothes, and putting me into his bed.

We hadn't even eaten, but neither of us mentioned it. He tucked himself in behind me, and though we were both very naked, neither of us made a move to take things further.

I stared at the navy blue walls of his bedroom, with Nate's arms tight around me, and replayed the moment in the elevator over and over. His breathing slowed into the peacefulness of sleep, while my brain wouldn't shut up. I'd done it again. Laid myself bare for him, though this time it had been emotionally, not physically.

And he'd rejected it.

I couldn't make this man love me. But I refused to be ashamed of how I felt. I wasn't that seventeen-year-old girl anymore. I wasn't going to run and hide or be angry that he didn't want me the way I wanted him.

I loved him. That was all there was to it. And when I put him on that bus tomorrow, I'd kiss him goodbye, and my heart would break.

I'd taken a chance. At least I could go on with my life, without wondering about the what-ifs.

I barely slept. I heard Molly every time she woke up, and the lullabies Shep's mom sang as she put her back to sleep. I counted Nate's trophies, all forty-six of them, lined up on rows of shelves, his true passion right there like a blinding light I couldn't turn off. I braced myself for the morning, willing the time to slow down so I could stay in the warmth of his embrace.

Dawn still came too soon. I dressed slowly in the clothes I'd worn yesterday, and perched on the end of Nate's bed while he threw his handful of belongings into the single bag he took on tour.

"Yesterday, before we got on the elevator, it was my boss on the phone." He tugged at the zipper on his bag without looking at me. "One of the other guys is out with an injury. It puts me in a great position to take his place on the leaderboard. I could win the entire season."

"That's great. I mean, not about the injury...but about taking the lead."

He nodded. "Yeah, I guess. They've booked a bunch of press for me to do. One of the morning TV shows and everything."

True happiness filled me. I wanted this for him. I wanted him to fulfill his dreams. This could be his big break. "Make sure you text me and let me know when it's on. I'll be watching."

He bit his lip. "Yeah, okay." His gaze strayed to the time on his phone. "I need to go. The bus will be at the stop in twenty minutes."

I stood with a nod and followed him out to the living room. I watched while he said goodbye to Shep's parents, kissing Mrs. Shepherd on the cheek and shaking hands with her husband. My heart damn near exploded as he picked up Molly, who gave him a wide smile.

"Gonna miss your squishy face, little girl. You'll probably be huge by the time I get home again."

Molly leaned in toward him with her mouth wide open and planted it on his cheek. Her chubby hands patted his nose and the side of his head.

He grinned at her. "You finally like me enough for kisses, right as I'm leaving?"

She just laughed at him.

Shep's parents did, too, but I could only smile weakly. Watching Nate hold Molly like that was like my future being dangled in front of me, then cruelly ripped away. It was all I could do to remain on my feet and not run crying from the house.

Nate passed the baby back to her grandparents and loaded his bag into the back of my car. I slid behind the wheel, blinking rapidly to keep the tears at bay, and managed to smile brightly when he got into the passenger seat beside me.

"One trip to the bus stop, coming up." I completely overdid it on the fake cheerfulness.

Nate noticed and glanced over at me unhappily. "Hallie..."

I couldn't look at him anymore. "Yeah?"

He sighed. "I want to be selfish and ask you to do the long-distance thing. But I also know it wouldn't be fair. I might be on the road for years. And you have a life here. A beautiful, big life, full of your friends, and that amazing house that will be a huge success. I don't want to be the weight that drags you down."

I shook my head rapidly. "You wouldn't be. We could FaceTime. And I could fly out sometimes..."

But even as I said it, we both knew it wouldn't work. Not when there was no light at the end of the tunnel. If he'd only had a year or two left, then maybe. But his career was indefinite at this point. And there was no sign of him settling down anytime in the near future.

That wasn't any way to live, no matter how much I loved him.

I pulled up at the bus stop, the tires of my old green Volkswagen kicking up the dust at the side of the road. Nate got out to get his bag, and I followed slowly. I eyed the highway that led into town, and my stomach lurched when in the distance, a hulking silver bus trundled toward us.

We both just stood there and watched it get closer with every passing second. I couldn't take my eyes off it, until it stopped right in front of us. Windows opened, and Nate's friends stuck their heads out, hooting and hollering.

Nate grinned, waving them back inside the bus.

He picked up his bag and slung it over his shoulder. "Hallie, look at me."

I didn't want to. I didn't want to show him the raw hurt and devastation in my eyes. But I couldn't deny him. I gazed up at him, letting him see it all.

He traced a finger down the side of my face. "You're amazing," he said softly. "You're beautiful, and smart, and you're gonna make some guy the happiest man in the world."

I smiled stiffly. "But that man isn't you."

The agony in his expression nearly did me in.

"I want to kiss you goodbye, but I don't want to hurt you anymore than I already have."

I nodded. It was for the best. If he took me in his arms now, I might never let go. And I could already see his boss frowning at him from inside the bus. So instead of pushing up onto my toes and kissing the man I'd fallen for all over again, I pulled back and offered him a wave, as if we were barely more than strangers.

Then I watched him get on a bus and leave me behind in a cloud of dust.

23

NATE

I trudged up the bus stairs, hating myself with every inch of my being, and so utterly miserable that I could barely breathe.

I'd boarded without telling Hallie how I felt. Because it had seemed the kinder thing to do, after I'd already hurt her so much. How unfair was it for me to tell her I loved her, right as I walked out of her life? The raw pain in her eyes had been the final straw that clamped my lips shut.

I wouldn't do it. I'd love Hallie Ryan until my dying day. I knew that, with something deep and gut-wrenching and *final.* A full-body conviction that I'd just let the best thing to ever happen to me slip away. I'd come back next Christmas and watch her with her new boyfriend. The next year they'd be married. Then one day, when I came back again, still blue with the knowledge she was with someone else, I'd see her happy, with her husband and children. She'd stop me and smile, and we'd maybe reminisce about those few days we'd had, where a fling had felt like forever. She'd go on with her life, and I'd go straight back to hating myself for ever letting her go.

Brad clapped me on the shoulder. "Listen, kid. The *Today* interview is in less than twenty-four hours. We're headed straight to the hotel in Texas, and you'll Skype in. Do you have any photos of your niece? Or your sister?"

I frowned at him. "Why?"

Brad looked confused. "Well, they're going to want to talk about the crash. This is your big comeback. People love a family tragedy. It'll make your wins all the sweeter. Maybe we can get your sister and brother-in-law in the stands for the next round..."

"My brother-in-law is still laid up in a hospital bed, and my sister is in a cast up to her hip. Neither of them can even leave the hospital, and you want to get them to a rodeo? Just for publicity?"

Brad folded his arms across his chest. "You know how the game is played here. It's not enough to be a good rider anymore. You want the sponsorship deals and the big money? You gotta give people more than your talent on the back of the bull. What about that girl you were with out there? Who's she? Girlfriend? You're gonna have to call that off. The female fans are going to want you single. Handsome boy and all."

I gaped at him. I'd heard about the PR stunts this guy pulled to get our sport in the media and fill seats at stadiums. But he'd had bigger riders to concentrate on, so I'd never seen it firsthand. Until now. Now I was it. And this was my new life?

No.

"What's that?" Brad asked.

I didn't even realize I'd spoken out loud. But I must have. "I said no."

"No, what?" The man seemed truly confused.

But suddenly I wasn't. Suddenly everything was as clear

as day, and I was making the biggest mistake of my life. "Stop the bus," I yelled to the driver.

"What?" Brad pushed to his feet. "What are you doing? Keep driving!"

The driver looked over his shoulder at us in confusion but didn't slow down. I grabbed my bag and stormed down the aisle. "Stop the bus," I said again.

This time, the man listened. He put his foot on the brake, and we rolled to a halt.

"You can't leave!" Brad shouted, the entire bus staring at us. "You wanted this! You signed a contract!"

"Then sue me. Because maybe I did want this at one point in my life. But I don't anymore." I stared Brad in the eye. "I quit."

Shocked murmurs rippled around the bus, but then the door was opening, and I was outside again, sucking in deep lungfuls of fresh clean air and feeling like I finally could breathe again.

I spun around to where I'd left Hallie and found her gaping at me in astonishment. We'd barely travelled five hundred yards, and I hurried toward her, picking up the pace until I was flat-out sprinting. I dropped my bag, lightening my load, and skidded in the dust to stop in front of her.

She stared up at me. "What's going on?"

I grinned at her. "I quit."

Her eyes widened. "You what? No, you did not. Get back on that bus and tell your boss you hit your damn head, or that you're high and can't be held accountable for the ridiculous words that just came out of your mouth."

"Nope. Can't do that, Hallie. Sorry. I quit. And I meant it."

She huffed out a frustrated breath. "Winning that title is your dream. And you're closer than ever."

It was all so clear to me now. I just had to make her see it, too. "It *was* my dream. It was the dream of a small-town, eighteen-year-old kid who thought the world began outside the county lines. I'd never been anywhere or done anything. But now I have. I've been all over the world. I've had people cheer my name. I've won awards, and made enough money to do whatever I want, at least for a while. Unless of course they sue me, which they probably will, judging from the expression on Brad's face right now. But I don't care."

"But the title..."

"Is a belt buckle. Nothing more. And I don't want it. Not anymore. I've been happier here with you, and my family, and out at Frost's ranch than I've been in a very long time out on the road. I want to come home."

She clamped a hand over her mouth, her eyes wide.

I pulled her into my arms. "I want to come home, and I want to build a life here. With you. I love you, Hallie. I have for a long time, and I was just too stupid to see what was right under my nose. I don't want to spend every day missing you, when I could be right here beside you."

"But what will you do?"

I shrugged. "I'll ask Frost for a job. Or I'll work on your house with you. I don't know. I just know that I don't want to ride anymore. I don't want a tour. I want a home. A relationship. I want you."

Without even thinking about it, I dropped down on one knee, in the dust on the side of the road, with a bus full of cowboys watching on in stunned silence. "Marry me, Hallie. I don't have a ring, because I didn't plan this, but I love you, and I want you to be my wife."

Hallie's mouth fell open. "Are you insane?"

I laughed. "Yeah, maybe. But I mean it." I glanced over my shoulder at the bus stopped down the road.

My friends had all piled out of the bus and were standing in a group, huge grins across their faces. "Get her, Nate!" somebody yelled, making me chuckle.

I turned back to Hallie. "Now's your chance to get me back," I whispered. "You could turn me down in front of all these people."

A tiny smile crept across her face. "I could, but I'm not as slow as you."

I grinned. "So is that a yes?"

She launched herself at me, sending my sprawling back into the dirt. "It's a yes, cowboy. It's a big hell yes."

I let out a whoop of delight and wrapped my arms around her, pulling her mouth down to mine. And when I kissed her, I knew it right to my soul.

This cowboy was home.

EPILOGUE

DOMINIC

Squished into the backseat of a tiny Volkswagen Beetle, with Summer Hunt pressed against my side, was agony in more ways than one. At six foot four, my legs were not made for small spaces, and my knees rammed Hallie in the back. But she didn't seem to notice. She smiled happily across the stick shift at Nate, who she'd let drive her car, her fingers combing through the hair at the nape of his neck.

The two of them were disgustingly happy, making lovesick eyes at each other when they thought no one was watching.

They were at complete odds with the couple crammed into the backseat with me.

Austin sat on the other side of Summer, glued to his phone. While Summer stared straight ahead, gazing out the windshield. She barely moved, her breathing deep and regular.

I nudged her. "You nervous?"

She started from her trance and glanced my way.

Fuck, she was beautiful. Every time she turned those big

brown eyes in my direction my heart slammed against my chest. This was why sitting so close to her was such agony for me.

All I wanted to do was kiss her. Bite her bottom lip, slide my tongue over her mouth and taste her. Plus more. There was so much more I wanted to do with her.

"Summer, look at this apartment. It would be perfect for us."

Austin's voice was like a bucket of cold water over my head.

Without answering my question, Summer turned to her dickhead of a boyfriend and peered over his shoulder at his phone.

"Apartment?" I questioned, straining to see as well.

Summer's floral scent filled my nose, and I backed off quickly before I did something stupid, like run my nose up her neck and whisper in her ear how good she smelled.

"Where is that?" Summer asked. "There's no apartment buildings around here."

Austin scoffed. "Of course not. There's nothing but cows around here. It's in the city. Not that far really. Only about a two-hour drive."

"Two hours?"

I frowned. "You're moving away?"

She shook her head while Austin nodded.

Austin glanced at her, his face filling with frustration. "You said you'd consider it."

Summer's body went rigid beside me. "I said I'd consider it if I didn't make the pro tour."

Austin waved his hand around. "Right, yeah. Whatever." He went back to searching apartment listings, his thumb flicking over his phone screen rapidly.

I clamped my teeth together as Summer returned to

staring out the window, completely withdrawing into herself again. She'd agreed to move in with this dickhead? I mean, I could understand that. From what I'd heard in snatches of conversations between our parents, she'd been with him ever since their high school prom. She was twenty-two. It was understandable she'd want a place of her own.

But the city? That wasn't Summer. Hell, I barely knew her, only getting to see her every couple of years when my family came out to Georgia to visit. But Summer was a small-town girl through and through. Her life was these bulls and the riding school she helped her father run. She fit in the city about as well as I did. Which was not at all. The place gave me hives.

As did Austin, and his smarmy fucking attitude. Had he seriously written Summer off before she'd even begun? If he thought she wasn't making the pros then he was about to be proven wrong. Pushing my luck, I put my hand on her arm and squeezed it before quickly moving it away. She glanced over at me, and our gazes collided.

Doubt clouded hers, and that made me want to reach across and strangle her boyfriend. Because it was him who had put that doubt there. Nobody else in her life doubted her ability for one second.

"Hey," I said softly, my voice barely audible over the grumble of Hallie's car engine and the radio playing. "You're going to nail this ride today. And you're going to make the pros next year. It's your time. I know it."

A tiny smile lifted the corner of her mouth. "Thanks."

I knew my words hadn't really helped her any. But I couldn't let her go out in that arena, without reminding her that at least one person in this back seat was rooting for her to succeed.

We pulled up in the dirt lot of the arena. It was just a

small outdoor one, nothing like the places she'd ride when she made the pros. But there was a big crowd already milling, waiting for the gates to open. This was one of the qualifiers for the next pro tour, and people wanted to see the young guns fighting it out.

We all piled out of the car, and Hallie and Nate both hugged Summer and wished her good luck. I didn't know her well enough to hug her, but I gave her a grin and nodded at her. I'd already said my piece in the car. We all turned to Austin, and for Summer's sake, I wanted him to step up. I wanted him to kiss her and tell her she was going to nail it.

He jabbed a finger into his phone and then put it to his ear. "Gotta call this real estate broker, babe. They might be able to get us a viewing this weekend."

"I've got to go," Summer told him. "I need time to get ready."

Austin nodded distractedly. "Sure, babe. Go. I'll see you after." He gave her a one-armed hug, but whoever he was calling must have answered the phone, because then he was stalking off, asking something about bathroom fixtures and bedroom sizes.

Summer watched him go for half a second, then spun on her heel and took off in the direction of the bucking chutes.

Hallie's face morphed from sunshine and smiles to seething anger. "It's a good thing Austin walked off before I punched him in his face."

I blinked at her. "You don't like him?"

"Do you? Does anyone? You heard him just now. I can't stand the way he treats her."

She wasn't the only one.

"Let's just go before he comes back. Maybe we can lose him in the crowd and not have to sit with him." Nate threaded his fingers through Hallie's, and I followed the two of them toward the stands. We weren't lucky enough to lose Austin completely, and he caught up to us as we sat down. I was the dumb fool who had to sit next to him.

"That apartment sounds so good," he said to me, as if I was actually interested. "Summer is going to love it."

He didn't know his girlfriend at all.

Or maybe he did, and he just didn't care.

The loudspeaker crackled to life, announcing the first rider, and a jolt of anticipation shot through me when I realized it was Summer. Hallie, Nate, and I all jumped to our feet and hooted and hollered.

Austin barely lifted his gaze. "Oh, she's first?" He looked at his watch. "Awesome. Maybe we can get out of here early and get some proper food for dinner."

Hallie stared at him.

But I was fucking done being polite. "Are you for real?"

"Huh?" Austin frowned at me.

"No seriously, are you for real right now? Your girlfriend is possibly about to make history, by becoming the first woman on the WBRA tour, and you don't even give a shit?"

"How is that any of your business?" Austin eyed me like I was a piece of trash. "You don't know anything about Summer. I don't even know why you're here."

I balled my fingers into fists, and it took everything in my power not to smash one into Austin's face. The only thing that stopped me was that Summer was getting on the back of her bull and I didn't want to miss her ride when security threw me out.

I also hated that he was right. It wasn't my business. I was barely even Summer's friend, so it wasn't my place to have an opinion on her dickwad partner.

Nate clamped a hand down on my shoulder. "Okay, my

friend. You're going to sit over here now." He guided me to the other side of him, so he and Hallie were both between me and Austin. I sat down hard, fuming, but focused on Summer.

We'd scored the front row, and I was grateful for it now, because it meant there was a metal barrier in front of me that I could white-knuckle. This ride wasn't the be all and end all for her. There would be other chances to qualify, but she needed to ride consistently well. At the very least, she needed to hang on for the eight seconds and get points on the board.

She shifted forward, her fingers clenched around the ropes. Then she nodded.

The gates flew open, and the timer started.

"She looks good!" Nate yelled, shifting his weight forward on the seat to grab the railing, just like I was.

She didn't just look good. She looked fucking perfect. Her form was amazing, and she was so clearly Kai Hunt's daughter. She rode just like he did, and he'd been one of the greats.

Summer would be better. I could already see it. One day, she'd break all her father's records.

"Go, go, go!" Hallie screamed.

I had no idea what Austin was doing. I couldn't take my eyes off his girl to find out.

His girl.

The thought curdled my stomach. He didn't deserve her. He had no respect for her talent.

One day I'd make her realize that.

The bull spun in the opposite direction, and Summer corrected, managing to hang on, though she slipped to one side.

I glanced at the clock. Two seconds to go.

"Come on!" I yelled.

The bull spun again, sending Summer listing even farther.

My heart hammered against my chest. She just had to hold on!

The buzzer sounded, and we jumped to our feet, cheering her name right along with the rest of the crowd.

The bull kicked out, and Summer went flying off his back, landing in the dirt.

The bull's hooves came down right on top of her.

And a scream of agony echoed through the suddenly silent arena.

TO BE CONTINUED... Preorder Dominic and Summer's swoon worthy romance here. Coming January 18th, 2021.

Want more hot, dirty talking cowboys while you wait? The original generation, including Frost and Addie's romance, starts with Talk Dirty, Cowboy. Read on for a sneak peek!

SNEAK PEEK AT TALK DIRTY, COWBOY. AVAILABLE NOW!

"He's a single dad and a dirty talking cowboy. I didn't stand a chance."

"Lily? What's wrong?" I knelt in front her tiny five-year-old body and scanned her for any obvious sign of injury. She seemed okay—no bleeding wounds or bones at odd angles. A little of my mommy panic ebbed away.

She shook her blonde head sadly, then whispered, "I don't feel so good."

I didn't even have time to flinch before she hurled her dinner up.

All over me.

I scrunched my eyes and mouth shut, whipping my head away just in time to miss the second wave, which landed all over her, the carpet, and again, me.

As her heaving was replaced with sobbing, I dared to survey the carnage. And oh, as soon as I opened my eyes, I wished I hadn't. Because it was bad. So very bad.

"Sorry, Momma," Lily whispered, tears rolling down her cheeks.

I gathered her shaking form up in my arms and recoiled when I touched her burning-hot skin. Whoa. Where had that fever come from? I held her for a moment, debating my options, then decided that the first order of business was getting both of us in a shower.

The doorbell rang when I was halfway down the stairs with my vomit-covered parcel. "Aiden! Could you grab that, please?"

I shifted Lily's weight, peering over her and carefully watching the stairs to be sure I didn't fall. Because wouldn't that just top this evening off. A vision of Lily and me rolling down the stairs, spreading puke everywhere as we went, flashed through my mind and I almost laughed. It was either that or cry.

I took the last step, landing in the living room, right as Aiden screamed, "Mom! It's for you!"

I froze.

Bowen, all six foot something of delicious, clean, and rugged man, stood in my foyer.

"Hello, Paisley."

ALSO BY ELLE THORPE

The Only You series (complete)

*Only the Positive (Only You, #1) - Reese and Low.

*Only the Perfect (Only You, #2) - Jamison.

*Only the Truth - (Only You, bonus novella) - Bree.

*Only the Negatives (Only You, #3) - Gemma.

*Only the Beginning (Only You, #4) - Bianca and Riley.

*Only You boxset

*All of Him - A single dad anthology, featuring Only the Lies. Only the Lies is a bonus, Only You novella.

Dirty Cowboy series (complete)

*Talk Dirty, Cowboy (Dirty Cowboy, #1)

*Ride Dirty, Cowboy (Dirty Cowboy, #2)

*Sexy Dirty Cowboy (Dirty Cowboy, #3)

*25 Reasons to Hate Christmas and Cowboys (a Dirty Cowboy bonus novella, set before Talk Dirty, Cowboy but can be read as a standalone, holiday romance)

Saint View High series (Reverse Harem, Bully Romance)

*Devious Little Liars (Saint View High, #1)

*Dangerous Little Secrets (Saint View High, #2)

*Twisted Little Truths (Saint View High, #3)

Buck Cowboys series (Spin off from the Dirty Cowboy series)

*Buck Cowboys (Buck Cowboys, #1)

*Buck You! (Buck Cowboys, #2)

Add your email address here to be the first to know when new books are available!

www.ellethorpe.com/newsletter

Join Elle Thorpe's readers group on Facebook!

www.facebook.com/groups/ellethorpesdramallamas

ACKNOWLEDGMENTS

I hope you loved Nate and Hallie's story. A big thanks first of all to my readers group and newsletter subscribers for choosing all sorts of aspects of this book, from Nate and Hallie's names, to Hallie's car. (Sian, I believe it was you who requested a green Volkswagen Beetle named Rylee! Lol)

Come join my readers group and my newsletter for more fun ways to be involved in future books, giveaways, and so I can get to know you better.

Thank you to Jolie Vines, Zoe Ashwood, Emmy Ellis and Karen Hrdlicka who make up my stellar editing team. And an extra thanks to Jo and Zoe for being my author besties too! Thank you to Sara Massery for the chats, sprints, and graphic design advice. Thank you to Dana and Louise for your early feedback. A massive thank you to my promo and review team for always being there for me.

And as always, a huge thank you to my family. To Jira, Thomas, Flick, and Heidi. You four are the loves of my life and I couldn't do any of this without you. How about that move to the country, huh? I've got more cowboy books to write and where better to write them than in the middle of nowhere? Let's make it happen!

Love, Elle x

ABOUT THE AUTHOR

Elle Thorpe lives on the sunny east coast of Australia. When she's not writing stories full of kissing, she's a wife and mummy to three tiny humans. She's also official ball thrower to one slobbery dog named Rollo. Yes, she named a female dog after a dirty hot character on Vikings. Don't judge her. Elle is a complete and utter fangirl at heart, obsessing over The Walking Dead and Outlander to an unhealthy degree. But she wouldn't change a thing.

You can find her on Facebook or Instagram(@ellethorpe-books or hit the links below!) or at her website www.ellethorpe.com. If you love Elle's work, please consider joining her Facebook fan group, Elle Thorpe's Drama Llamas or joining her newsletter here. www.ellethorpe.com/newsletter

facebook.com/ellethorpebooks
instagram.com/ellethorpebooks
goodreads.com/ellethorpe
pinterest.com/ellethorpebooks

CPSIA information can be obtained
at www.ICGtesting.com
Printed in the USA
BVHW031633310821
615695BV00001B/230